Prodigal Ex

THE FALL FROM GRACE SERIES

THERESA PAPA

AMPAPA L.L.C.

PRODIGAL EX

ISBN- 979-8-9851498-0-7 (Ebook)

ISBN- 979-8-9851498-3-8 (Paperback)

Library of Congress Control Number: 2024910771

Created with Vellum

One

GEMMA BLOOM

Do you think we can deliberately fuck up our fate by the poor decisions we make? And when we engage in these reckless decisions, do we lose a little of our God given graces? I don't think it's absurd to believe that we're not responsible for the direction our lives take. But to an extent, not every second is predestined or written in the stars. Some things have to be random. Our choices change the trajectory of events. But maybe there's some symbolic scroll somewhere out there where every step, every relationship, all our accomplishments and defeats, are written. Does it laugh when we try to change things? And then, does it merely bring about us coming full circle face to face with our fate once again?

Eleven years ago… Age 18

"Gem, it's your turn. Get out there!" My best friend, Dayo, just finished.

I take the last shot in the lineup on the desk and gulp it down. "Coming."

The club is dark except for the stage where the spotlights are all on me. I can only see the faces in the front row. The usual regulars money in hand. A heady mix of cologne, sweat, and alcohol fills the air as always in club Go Down in Flames. We call it the Flame for short.

My body instinctively moves to the pulsating beats of the music. An erotic dance to excite the patrons and make them want to spend more money. The pole is my only dance partner, a skill I perfected over time, toning my body. A lean yet curvy figure, taut abdominals, well-defined arms and legs, and large voluptuous breasts. My costume (picture my air quotes) comprises a bedazzled thong and pasties. I change it up daily with different gemstone colors.

"Gemstone, over here. I got some Benjamins for ya!"

Jimmy is a nightly visitor, and old enough to refer to money by nicknames. He keeps me clothed in my real life with his one-hundred-dollar bills. I shimmy over to him and he does his usual flirting while inserting the money into my thong. Overall, harmless men who are looking to escape the mundane of their lives fill the club. But once in a while, there's that one asshole who shows up and fucks up everything.

"Why don't you come over here? Cunt. I got only ones, but that shouldn't matter. Get that ass moving right in front of me."

I do a few moves to appease the sick fuck and not to start a commotion.

"Don't call her that, you asshole," Jimmy gets in the guy's face.

"She's here for my entertainment. I can fucking call her whatever I want." One punch and Jimmy is on the floor. As I try to climb down from the stage to help him, the fucker lunges and wraps my ponytail around his fist. He jerks my head back, making me fall into his lap.

All motion ceases. The guy unwraps the hand from my hair and pushes me off his lap. I spin around to find my savior with a blade at his throat, whispering in his ear. Asshole's eyes are as big as saucers and it looks like he just fuckin peed himself.

At last, two of the club's bouncers flank asshole and drag him away after the dark-haired, muscular man lets him go. He steps into the light, and with only his fingertips, touches my arm. "Are you okay?"

I look down at his hand. "Yes, thank you for stepping in. I can't understand why the doormen didn't come earlier." I love powerful hands, so sexy.

He exudes self-assurance without appearing arrogant. His eyes are dark and expressive, conveying vitality and warmth. A sturdy jawline with chiseled cheekbones matches the rest of the package below. His physique is broad shouldered, with a wide expanse of pectorals in between. The guy works out religiously.

"That guy is drunk past the line of decorum, even for a place like this one." He notices my stare at his hand and removes it, running his fingers through his chin length chestnut hair. The movement confirms my previous thoughts when his well-formed biceps flex under his T-shirt sleeves. "Uh, no offense."

"None taken. Can you help me back up?" I nod to the stage.

He smiles with straight white teeth, picks me up like I weigh nothing, and deposits me back up on the platform. There's no gawking at my boobs or touching my ass. He's the perfect gentleman. This place never brings in a guy like him.

"Thanks."

He nods as Jimmy yells for another round to water down his broken ego. When I look back towards the stranger, he's gone.

The club returns to the previous vibe from before the altercation. I finish my dance nine-hundred dollars richer. Jimmy was extra generous tonight. Back in the dressing room, Dayo, stage name Diamond, already dressed in her street clothes and waiting for me to finish.

"What went on out there? You know you should never leave the stage, girl. It's dangerous."

"Yeah, but Mikey and Philly were nowhere near us. I felt Jimmy needed help. He's old."

"And your own personal ATM." She giggles and slaps my bare ass as I walk by.

"I won't deny that he keeps food on my table." I put my sweatshirt on, not bothering to remove my pasties. Then I pull on my jeans, boots, and winter coat. We make our way out the alley door into the early dawn light.

Dayo lets me sleep on her couch when I need a place to crash. Thank goodness, because it's twenty below outside and a warm place is a necessity. Exotic dancers in a run-down backstreet club don't make enough to pay rent in the city of Chicago. I'm homeless at the moment. If it weren't for good friends and people like Jimmy tipping me, I'd be fucked. I'm saving for an apartment, but scrounging up first and last months' rent, along with a security deposit, is daunting. The most important thing is trying to stay alive right now.

"Let's not wake Bo. He's working later today," Dayo says of her husband sleeping in the other room.

"I'll be asleep as soon as my tits hit the sofa. Goodnight."

Coffee aroma wafts under my nose as I open one eye. Dayo is holding the cup. "Oh my gosh, thank you." I take the cup and cheers her.

She sits in the recliner across from my temporary bed. We never talk about when I'll move out, but I have plans.

"Bo already leave for work?" She nods. "Are you sure he's OK with me crashing here, Day?"

"He's fine. Work keeps him away all day and we're at the club at night, so you'll never even cross paths."

"I'll make it up to you guys someday. I promise."

She flaps her wrist at me. "No worries, my girl."

The sun shining through the window highlights Day's beautiful features and dark brown skin tone. She was born in Nigeria and once shared with me that her name signifies 'arrival of joy' in Yoruba. One of the many languages spoken in her native country. She and her husband Bo, short for Bolaji, have been married for five years.

We spend the morning chatting and then go to the gym to get in our workout. I manage to snag free passes from the manager, a regular at the Flame.

On Monday, it's slow, just the way I like it. The men that are there always ogle us when we walk in. I guess the contrast between my blond, blue-eyed features and Day's dark exotic ones capture their attention. Regina always meets us here and right on cue, she steps out of the locker room.

"Hey, bitches! You ready to get your sweat on?" She motions with her eyes at the hot guy on the Peloton. I swear she picks up random guys anywhere.

"Hey Ray, are you working tonight?" Day asks.

Regina hops on a digital bike next to hot guy and the virtual trainer pops up on the screen. "Yeah, are you?"

"No, but Gem needs a ride. You got her?"

Ray nods, and I mouth a thank you to her. Then she goes to work talking up the hot guy. He smiles and takes his earbuds out to talk.

Today's the day I conquer the weight room since it's almost empty. I prefer not to deal with all the sweaty guys in there on busy days. It can get kinda gross with all the machines full of sweat. Day waves me on and gets on her treadmill. Once on the first machine, I notice a stunning man walk out of the locker room, straight toward the weight room.

Our eyes meet and I can feel my brows raise in surprise. It's him! My savior from last night is here in the flesh. And Ohhh how sexy that flesh is in his shorts and tank top. The biceps I imagined last night under his shirt are on full display, making me want to bite them.

"Hey, it's you. Gemstone? Right?"

"Gemma, Gemma Bloom."

He reaches for my hand to shake it. "Billy Dedano." These hands won't let me sleep. They're all I can think about.

"Nice to meet you formally. Thanks again for last night."

"It was my pleasure to save a beautiful lady, just trying to do her job." The whole fucking room lights up when he smiles.

I realize I've stopped mid reps and start over, while he takes the free weights off their stand, puts in his earbuds, and begins. How am I not gonna ogle him the entire time? It's more of a workout than the weights. OK, breathe in and out, in and out. If there's one thing I know, it's in and out, in and out. My dirty mind always makes me giggle.

After some time goes by, Day pokes her head in. Billy's back is to me defined and strong as hell. So, I just go with Day and leave him to his workout.

Two

BILLY DEDANO

Eleven years later…

The elevator doors open to the lower level, where I keep my most prized possessions. I'm a collector of cars. These aren't your average vehicles you see on the road; they are the most expensive in the world. I have a list … a bucket list of models I aim to acquire in my lifetime. In this chapter in my life, I'm halfway there if I kept myself from adding to the lineup. The Bugatti La Voiture Noire is the most coveted and priciest car right now. I'm also really into th*e world's most* expensive car ever made. The Rolls-Royce Boat Tail.

When the movement sensing lights turn on in the temperature regulated garage, the polished floors come into view. But so does the carnage.

"What the fuck, Billy!" Joe says.

My eyelids squeeze together, and I shake my head. "She did it again."

"Don't tell me … Gemma did this?" He waves his hands.

"She's trying to get my attention in the worst way possible. Besides showing up at all my clubs drunk out of her ass, she also pulls stunts like this. Her obsession with a certain country music star and a particular song gave her this idea."

Joe's eyes go wide. "Did you fuckin cheat on her? That's one place I draw the line. I will never be a cheater. Hence, I've deemed myself the eternal bachelor."

I pick up the hammer my wife left on the floor. "No, man, she's an attention whore. You know how busy I am with all the bullshit that goes on in the clubs. She tired of sitting at home waiting for me. I told her to fucking get a hobby or something. You would think a girl that I found practically living on the street would want to go out and spend some of her billionaire husband's money. Not my bride! She left, taking only what she brought. I didn't even know she still had that shit."

"This is just too fucked up. You've been separated for almost two years. Are you having me draw up the divorce papers soon?" Joe's head swivels back and forth as he surveys the damages.

"Fuck, no! I don't know. I had her sign some bullshit contract and made her think we got divorced two years ago. She never reads anything, and I was desperate to get her off my back." I massage the kink in my neck.

He stops dead in his tracks and holds up his right hand. "Stop talking. I don't want to know the details of how you committed fraud. I know nothing of any fake papers, you got it?"

Joe is not only my best friend from childhood, he's my lawyer. He is great at what he does. Which is why I introduced him to all my billionaire buddies and made him a shitload of money. He now owns his own firm and mingles with us in the same social circles. Determined to remain a confirmed bachelor, he does well with the ladies. It seems he has it all figured out because he never has issues like the one I'm dealing with. My Gemma. Color me envious.

"She took a hammer to the glass in your Bugatti, man. There's red paint on the finish of your Pagani Roadster! If that doesn't justify a reason to divorce her, I don't know what is."

"It's red lipstick, not paint." Gemma wrote, 'you ruined my life.' I don't understand how giving her the world on a proverbial platter can ruin anything. "She's an alcoholic and Maria fired her from Innamorare last year. She went back to dancing naked in one of my rival clubs. I bought the damn place to make sure she's taken care of." It's déjà vu, just like when I met her. "First, I had to come to terms with her becoming an escort. Maria and I had an arrangement: she'd focus on men seeking companionship, avoiding any sexual games. I mean, I'm not fuckin stupid. I know she's having sex with someone. But now, it's fucking misery to watch on the monitors while men touch her and gawk at her."

He pats me on the shoulder. "You got it bad! Seems to me you should find a way to get her back and give her what she wants or divorce her in reality."

I get a rag from the workbench and start rubbing off the lipstick. It's my favorite shade on those fuckable, suckable lips. I rub it between my thumb and index finger, reminiscing about looking down and seeing it on my cock after one of our fuck sessions. "Gemma is one in a million. I can't completely close the door on that. One day I'll get her back. I still just need to figure out how to do it."

"Hell, I'm the first guy to say women fuck up your life. However, when you're as obsessed with Gemma as you are, no other woman can meet those standards. And then, you find yourself fucking your hand instead of pussy thinking of only her. I've been in that boat and the only outcome was a sinking ship that almost caused me to drown." Joe removes his suit jacket and grabs the car wax. He buffs over the spots I removed the lipstick from. I grab the broom and start sweeping up the glass on the floor.

Reminiscing about the past, I lean on the broomstick. "She was so fucking easy to please in the beginning. Never asked for anything. Not like all the gold diggers I dated before her. She was simple and low maintenance. Who knew she'd go bat shit crazy after three years of dating on and off and six years of marriage?"

Joe laughs. "You mean four years of marriage? She thinks she's been single for the last two years. What were her exact words when she requested a divorce? Women always want to talk about stuff. There's your clue."

She had stated; I stopped paying attention. I focused solely on my business and the next conquest, leaving her by herself. She wanted me. That's all.

"She said that the worst thing in the world is not hate, it's indifference. Some shit like that." I throw the glass shards into the garbage bin.

Joe takes a big breath. "You better look long and hard at your life and set your priorities straight. Two years is a long time to let this go. The clubs almost run themselves and the new build in Dubai has Andy watching over it. You want Gemma back? You need to put it on your fucking goals calendar right in front of building an additional club in Vegas and a riverboat casino on Lake Michigan." He puts his jacket back on and pats me on the back. "I got a meeting. See you this weekend."

The elevator closes behind him and I deflate on my down filled sofa where I love to sit and admire my cars. Only today, I don't even see them as I remember the conversation when she told me she wanted a divorce.

Two years earlier…

"This isn't working anymore. I want a divorce." Gemma sits across the dinner table, her shoulders rounded, mixing and pushing her food around her plate with her fork. It's the third time she's mentioned divorce. I've been warned that my time is running out.

I pound my fist on the table. "What the Fuck! Gemma! You don't just say those words in dinner conversation. In fact, I never want to hear *that* word out of your mouth again."

"Now you're ordering me not to use certain words, like I'm one of your employees?" She drops her fork with a loud clang. "Divorce! I want one." She stands and her chair falls backward. Her piercing blue eyes slice my heart in two.

I lower my voice and check my emotions. "What fucking happened since this morning when we made love and now?"

"This morning we fucked like we do every morning because God forbid, I shake your routine. I let you get your rocks off and then turn over and go back to sleep. I'm merely a vessel for you to deposit your sperm." She takes off toward the stairs.

I follow, catching up after deflecting the foiled door slam. "Gem, honey, I don't want to fight. I'm too tired. Please, just tell me how to make it better."

"That's how you go through life, Billy … put a bandaid on it and make it better." Her voice drips with sarcasm. She pulls her dress over her head. "Can't you see I'm bleeding out here? There's nothing left of me. I have no identity! I have no purpose except to please you and get nothing in return." Her bra hits the floor, and she heads into the bathroom in just her thong panties.

I grab her by the waist and spin her around. Her breasts bounce against my chest. "What do you mean, nothing in return? I plucked you from living on your friend's sofa two steps from selling yourself on the street. I gave you everything any woman could ever want."

"You look down your nose at people with disdain who are forced to do things to survive. That's where I'm different. We see ourselves as the epitome of strength and sincerity. At least we're brutally honest with ourselves about why we do things. And there's no doubt we know what's important in life!" She presses her palms against my chest in an attempt to get away.

"Tell me, Gem. What's important? Educate me on life. Forgive me if I think it's important to have a warm, safe bed to sleep in and food in the refrigerator for three meals a day."

"Oh please! You hypocrite! As if you think those are the only necessities in life. What about the material possessions you add to on a daily basis? And don't get me started on the cars."

"It never bothered you before. Why now? You seriously want a divorce on the grounds that I'm a little too materialistic? We are the couple everyone else aspires to be."

Tears fall down her cheeks. "Pffft, I don't even aspire to be me right now. I'm a trophy on your proverbial shelf. The place where you store all the things people should envy. You never even talk to me. The only time we're face to face is when you're shoving your dick in me. Unless you decide you want to change it up and fuck me from behind. I've even told you twice before that I want a divorce and you brushed it off as well. A little too inconvenient, maybe?"

The sobering revelation hurts, so I let her go, letting my arms fall to my sides, my head down. "Haven't heard you complain about our sex life before."

"It was always amazing until you took on more with the new clubs in Vegas and Dubai. Pushing me, your wife, to the bottom of the list," she complains as she strips off her thong and turns on the shower before stepping inside.

Fuck if I'm gonna let my woman think sex with me is less than amazing. So, I drop my clothes on the bathroom floor and sneak in behind her in the enormous shower. When I slide my palms around her ribs and pull her into me, she melts. She tilts her head to allow my mouth better access to her neck. My fingertips slip into her and she lifts one leg to rest her foot on the bamboo bench. Moans escape her lips as I bring her to a shaking climax. Then I do it two more times after spinning her around, resting her back on the bench and spreading her wide for my mouth. She sits up, eyeing my stiff cock while her hands reach for it. Gemma is the best I've ever had, so I don't last long before I pull out of her mouth with a pop and slip inside her. She clings to me like she'll never let go. Yet, it's as if there's a goodbye in there somewhere.

It's been two months since Gemma left me. I couldn't deal with an actual divorce, so I lied to her. Faked the documents and had her sign. She's my wife and I'm fucking determined to get her back. Nevertheless, I need to discuss a recent concern at Ablaze. My manager tells me that Benjamin Wixx wants to see the owner. After a tiring shift at my new bar, Ice, I was planning to get some sleep at 2 am. However, I ended up going to my original club, The Flame, which I later renamed Ablaze and transformed into an exclusive VIP venue.

Benjamin Wixx is a fund manager for the rich and famous. Hell, I even think Joe has some of my funds invested in his firm. The guy's making millions for the investors, so everyone wants in on it. When people throw around large amounts of money, they tend to forget the past. Not me.

His name used to be Benny Stolo. He is, without a doubt, ten years older than me, but I remember what he did to my father. Benny wanted dad to launder cash through our bars for him. He tried to muscle him with some big beefy jerks and a threat. He didn't know that my dad was godfather to Guy Galanti's son. Galanti is still running things in the Chicago syndicate today, but from jail. My father's word brought unwanted visitors to Benny's door. They roughed him up a little, and he never bothered my family again.

As I check the mirror in my private bathroom next to my office. I can't help but wonder if Wixx or Stolo is out for a petty revenge. Maybe counting on the fact that he thinks I have a short memory? Or maybe he assumes since my father's retired, I never knew of the incident? Either way, he's messing with the wrong man. Muscle men aren't necessary for me to be threatening; I am the muscle and brains of this outfit.

Muscle building is an art I embraced early in my life and I'll continue to keep it up forever. I won Iron man competitions while building my sculpted physique. Strength comes from creating an imposing appearance and people respect it. Some people label us as gym rats. They're just jealous of our impeccable symmetry. I wash my hands, then sit at my desk, pressing the button to send in Wixx.

"What can I do for you, Mr. Wixx?" I gesture for the man to sit and he obliges. When I offer him an expensive cigar, he takes it and puts it into the chest pocket of his fucking custom-made suit. I prefer a casual look for everyday wear, but I have custom suits to accommodate my muscular torso. This idiot? He just wants to brag by wearing expensive suits as a uniform.

He sits crossing his leg with one foot over his knee, then smooths his hand over his pant leg. He wears more diamond rings than most women would. Up close, I notice he tweezes his eyebrows like a girl.

I pour two glasses of Scotch and he takes one. After a sip, he begins.

"This is a curtesy call to inform you I'll be throwing my hat in the ring as a club owner in direct competition with you." He sniffs. "We break ground one block south in two days. And I bought that Misty building that closed last year across the street from Ice."

"Wow, a direct hit on two of my Chicago clubs? What'd I do to deserve that?" I keep my cool and even smirk.

"It's just business, Dedano. I'm in the business of making money." He twirls one of his rings. "Maybe you want in on it? Partners?"

"Well, it's a free enterprise, Mr. Wixx, and money is made by having the best system. Mine is beyond masterful, down to the tiniest detail. Choose a spot, execute my system and viola success. I know I make it look easy. Many have failed in their attempts to duplicate it. But my businesses stand the test of time." I sip my drink before I continue to let that sink in. "You already know that, since you're here offering a partnership. I'm not interested in partnering with anyone. My businesses are thriving and will stay profitable."

"Like you did to Misty a year ago, I might just drive you out of business, Dedano. People gravitate to the newest trend. And my establishment will be it."

I toast him with my almost empty glass and finish it.

"Thanks for the heads up, Wixx. Might wanna finish that drink and get some sleep. You're showing your age. My father retired a few years ago. If I remember the history, you wanted to work with him as well. Enlighten me. Why is a guy on the edge of retirement jumping into a risky venture?" I had to at least get one dig in.

He stands, putting his empty glass on the desk. But he's smiling when he says, "Fuck you, Dedano, I got twenty years before I'm retirement age. We can't all be connected... I had to overcome many things by myself," he says, becoming pensive. "My mother needed expensive medical care at the time when your father squashed my deal." He waves his hand and disappears out the door.

I lean back in my chair, weary from a long day. One thing I'm sure of is that Benny Stolo is going to launder cash and sell drugs at his clubs. I always have my bouncers keep the drug dealers out and I sure as fuck wouldn't launder currency. I feel no threat, as I have financial interests worldwide. It will be interesting to witness the outcome.

Short on sleep and long on aggravation the next night, Gemma shows up to fuck with my head. She is here with her crew from Maria Capisi's Escort service. When I sit Ian and Andrew in the VIP section, I notice them getting more and more animated. As soon as I sit down to have a drink with my buddies, Gemma stumbles over and plops her ass in Ian's lap. Her long blond hair is on his face, her big blue eyes are bloodshot. He doesn't know who she is because they've never met. In the years I was married, Ian was missing from our group of friends dealing with his daughter's illness.

Gemma has been drinking too much and acting fucking stupid since she left me. She works as an escort to billionaires at Club Innamorare and she dances at another club I just bought. I couldn't let her work for the sleaze who owned it.

"You hot guys took the last bottle of excellent champagne." Gemma slurs to Ian. Annoyed, he unwraps her arms from around his neck and stands. Gemma steadies herself on my chair and I grab her arm. One of the male escorts from Gem's table gets in Ian's face and Ian punches him in the jaw. Gemma screams, so I throw her over my shoulder and gesture to the bouncers to get the other guy off the floor and follow me outside.

Once outside, I position Gem on her feet. She's pissed. "Fuck you, Dedano!" She swipes her hair out of her face.

She stumbles on her heels and reaches down to remove her shoes. I catch her before she face plants and whisper in her ear. "Funny, that's still your last name as well."

Three

GEMMA

Present day…

I left Billy and began working as an escort for Maria. She and I didn't see eye to eye on many things, including my drinking. It's not as if the job was conducive to staying away from liquor. She fired me a year ago. Returning to stripping wasn't difficult for me. Many people view becoming a stripper as a last resort, the final choice after exploring all other avenues. A desperate decision. That's such a huge misconception! All the people I've danced with are total badasses. Stripping allows you to earn a lot of money while only working a few days a week. This gives you the freedom to pursue other interests or education. I never did.

I've decided that I'm getting too old for this shit. I miss the days of when I made double the money at Innamorare. Who am I kidding? I loved the sex too. Anyway, little did I know, Maria's not the madam anymore at Innamorare. They had no idea who I was. It didn't feel comfortable there. How can I be certain if they do a thorough screening on the clients as Maria? So, I decided to bail.

Throughout my childhood, my friends have proven to be more dependable than my family. It's a big decision to throw away my pride and ask Angel for a job. She always had my back when we worked as escorts together. She's now in a blissful marriage, mother of twin toddlers, and stepmother to a ten-year-old little girl. I'm hoping she might hire me to help as a nanny.

Now, here I am in an opulent building on Lake Shore Drive. What is referred to as Chicago's Gold Coast, gifts in my hands for the twins. Angel has no idea what I'm about to ask. The elevator door opens. There stands Ang, looking radiant as ever.

"Gem! It's so nice to see you again. It's been way too long. I've missed you." Her arms envelope me in a firm hug. "Please step inside."

"I've missed you too, Ang. I wish I would've come earlier. Sorry, I wasn't returning your calls." I squeeze her forearm.

Angel swipes her other hand. "Don't mention it. I understand you were going through a difficult time."

She leads me to the foyer where in front of us is a balcony and floor to ceiling windows showcasing the most magnificent view of the city of Chicago I've ever seen.

"Wow, this is fabulous!" During my marriage to Billy, we lived in a lakeside mansion with a backyard. The views were just as amazing. But seeing skyscrapers up close at eye level is breathtaking.

"Thanks, we wrestle with the decision to move to a house with a backyard for the kiddos, like your house with … ugh." She slaps her own forehead. "Sorry, I didn't mean to bring up Billy five minutes into the conversation."

"It's okay. You were there to save me when I used to get drunk and frequent his club. I'm grateful for a friend like you. And I promise I stopped stalking him at work a while ago." I chuckle.

With a smile, she waves me into the living room where adorable twin boys sleep in a modern playpen. "The boys are napping. We prefer them napping amidst the hustle and bustle, avoiding the need to tiptoe around. They would sleep through an earthquake."

"I brought them each something." I hand the little gift bags to her. "They're just stuffed animals. I got them both the same to avoid any potential fights between the kids over which one they wanted."

"Thank you. That wasn't necessary. But they'll adore it." Her shoulders rise to her chin while she grins.

We head into the kitchen where she's set up a scrumptious-looking lunch. My stomach rumbles at the sight. I forgot to eat today. We sit and have sandwiches with brownies for dessert. I had forgotten the joy of having lunch with a friend. My only girlfriends socialize at the strip club, then we all go home to our regular lives.

"So how's Ian? You look happy, Ang." I smile.

"Call me Eve from now on." Her eyebrows scrunch together. "It's just in case my mother-in-law is around. My time as an escort is on the down low. Also, for my position at the hospital."

Dr. Eveangelina Pope is a respected pediatric oncologist here in Chicago and the entire country. I found out only after she married Ian. She treated his daughter for cancer. No one knew she was living a double life working at Innamorare. Including me.

"Oh, yes! Pfft, I understand. No problem, Eve." I take a bite of brownie.

"When Ian calls me Angel, everyone just thinks it's a pet name."

"You two were unexpected fate. Huh?"

She rises and pours me a cup of coffee. "That's the only thing you can call it. When I met him and Adelina at the hospital, I was in the dark in the literal sense, as to the man I slept with every week." We both crack up because Ian always blindfolded her when she was his personal escort.

"How is Adelina now?" I sip my coffee.

She puts her brownie down and lifts her cup. “She’s ten going on twenty-two. Lina’s a big help with the boys.” Eve sips her coffee.

“Speaking of the twins, do you have a nanny?” I wiggle in my seat a little.

“Yes, we do. She’s here on my days at work. Why do you ask?” Her brow cinches.

I look down, playing with my napkin. “I’m looking for work … So, I thought you might hire me.”

“Ahhh. Have you had experience with small children that I’m not aware of?”

“Um, no. But I love kids.” This is uncomfortable. “Maybe I shouldn’t have come.”

She laughs. “A nanny is not the position for you, Gem. Why aren’t you living off the fund Billy gave you in the divorce?”

The napkin in my hand twists into a knot. “I can’t. I want him to understand that I don’t need the extravagant things he overwhelmed me with during our marriage.”

“Gem, come on, what’s so bad about being rich? Just put the money part into perspective and live your life accordingly. Are you so dead set on making your point that you’d starve? What good would that be?”

I’m ashamed of my prideful way of handling Billy. My cheeks heat. “I’m aware it’s just pride and principles. But without those I have nothing, Eve.”

“I’m not passing any judgement, Gem. Remember, I love you and I comprehend where you came from. You’re one of the strongest people I know. The way you grew up is shitty. It was messed up when the same thing happened to you with Billy.”

“Thanks Eve, it means a lot coming from you.” I reach across and hug her. “Even after two years, I still long for him. I’ll always love him.”

"I know sweetie, I'm sorry."

"The bitterness and resentment I felt for him during the divorce has subsided. I tried to heal and be patient, to work on myself. Be my own advocate. It sucks to be alone in a world knowing your soulmate exists."

"Have you tried speaking with him? Maybe he'll get his head out of his ass and pay attention."

"I swore after my mother was indifferent to me my entire childhood that I would let no one else make me feel like that again. He engaged in it without thought and never comprehended that it was killing me more each day." Tears fall down my cheeks. "I was once again invisible."

"Oh, Gem, there's got to be a way to fix you two. What if he still loves you, but just made a mistake? Perhaps now that he's a billionaire twice over, he'll let go of his empire and take a step back." She has tears as well.

I shake my head in doubt. "After the last time he threw me out of his club, I got cleaned up. When Maria fired me, it was the last straw. I kind of dropped off everyone's radar. Got into a program for alcoholics. It was the hardest thing I've ever done besides leaving Billy. Working every day in bars and staying sober is almost impossible. But I did it. Now, I'm ready to step into something new."

"I might have the perfect placement for you." She licks her lips and picks up her phone.

"You do? Where?" I can feel my eyebrows peak.

"Well, have you been in touch with Maria?" I shake my head. "Her business placement service finds alternative jobs for escorts seeking a change. I'm sure she can find the perfect spot for you."

"I don't even have a high school diploma. How would I get a regular job?" My eyes roll.

"Let Maria worry about that part. I'll call her and see if she's busy."

Four

BILLY

Eleven years earlier…

The girl left before I could get her number. When I turned from doing my squats, she was gone. I've tried to stop thinking about her since she jumped off the stage the other night. She influenced my decision to buy that sleazy place in the small amount of time I spoke with her. I guess once I take over next month, I'll have all the information I need.

The decision to buy the Flame and turn it into a respectable club is the byproduct of my quest. My top priority is proving to my father that I can take over and further elevate the company's success.

"Where'd the two girls go?" My best friend, Joe, steps off the treadmill. He wipes the sweat off his face with his towel.

"Don't worry, you will see more of them anytime at my new place."

"Fuck, are they strippers?"

I nod, "like I said, much more of them."

"That sounds perfect. With all the studying I have. I'm lucky I found time for a workout."

"By next weekend, I'll have taken over the reins. We'll throw a party to celebrate."

"Right now, what I need is a party with those two beauties. Studying for the bar exam is kicking my ass."

"Yeah, I forgot what you look like in the past few months."

"It'll all be over this week. Two days of tests and boom, I'm a lawyer. Come the weekend, I'll be well-rested and ready to party."

All week I'm organizing and scheduling the workers to make Down in Flames into the sexy club where rich, successful people want to party. I'm adding a fresh coat of paint to the black walls and ceilings to get the classy vibe I'm going for. The rooms will be divided and repurposed into a formal dining room with a full kitchen, a library, a gaming room, and a sports room. Flames is getting an upgrade.

The weekend approaches, but with the huge dump of snow, there's not one customer at the club. Some girls called to report their buried cars, while others called to report being sick. The celebration I planned is just Joe, Gemma, Regina and me.

The impact of seeing Gemma again was something I hadn't planned. It's typical for me to establish the boss-employee dynamic as soon as I take over the business. I'm all over the place because of this girl. Yes, I couldn't help but imagine her on stage as I pleasured myself last week. But this girl's not just spank bank material. Somehow, she's crawled under my skin. I even fucking feel like I wanna protect her. What's up with that?

Gemma Bloom is my employee, but also my new obsession.

Five

GEMMA

The February weather warmed a few degrees, causing the skies to dump fourteen inches of snow on us. I can't afford to stay home from work just for weather reasons like Day. She and her hubby are snuggling in for a night of TV.

"Ray, I need a ride to work. Will your SUV make it through this?"

"Bob can get through anything. I'll be there to pick ya up."

Regina calls her car Bob. It all stemmed from one night on the icy roads where we were bobbing and weaving down Lake Shore Drive. The lake waves came close to reaching the street. Despite our fear, we kept our composure by joking about naming Regina's car Bob.

The drive tonight is long, but not as scary. Some streets aren't plowed as well as others. City of Chicago Streets and Sanitation are doing the best they can. A shiver runs through me as I trudge to the entrance of Flame with Ray. "Surprise, they plowed the parking lot. This never happened before." I gather my puffy coat tighter around me and pull open the door.

"No one is here." Regina plops her bag on one of the empty tables while I turn on the lights.

"I'll check the office. Rick must be here if it's unlocked."

I peel off my coat and scarf down to my sweater and jeans before heading down the dark hallway to the dressing rooms. On my left is Rick's office. I knock.

Upon opening the door, a man is sitting with his head down at the desk. But this is not Rick's bald, greasy noggin. This man is everyone's dream of luxurious, silky shoulder length hair. Billy looks up with those sexy brown eyes and smiles from ear to ear. I'm fucking rendered speechless.

"Your mouth's hanging open. I take it you weren't expecting to find me in this chair?"

I shake my head. "Come sit, I'll explain." He comes from around the desk, grabs my hand from my side, and leads me to sit. "I'm the new owner of the Flame." He says it matter-of-factly. "Hey, glad you got here safe and sound. But I don't think we'll require a show without customers."

"Uh, I have to get paid. Show or no show, you're gonna pay me. Right?" I cross my arms. "Not that I'm poor … But the couch cushions aren't giving up loose change too easily right now."

He grins. "Of course." He pulls out a bottle and pours two shots. "Here, have a drink. It'll warm you." I've never been known to turn down premium liquor, so I slam it.

There's a banging sound coming from the hallway. We both check the hallway and find Regina and a guy fucking around against the wall. From my angle, I can see that her jeans are unzipped, and he has his arm buried deep.

"Get a fucking room, Joe." Billy yells. The guy ignores him. He picks Ray up over his shoulder, causing her to screech. They disappear into the dressing rooms across the hall.

"They'll be busy for a while." I laugh. "Ray's a sexaholic with lots of stamina." Billy laughs with me, closing the door and resuming his seat. "What's the craziest place you've had sex?" *Why the hell did I just ask my new boss that question? Another shot, please.* As I hold out my glass, he fills it and his face lights up with a smile. I put my feet up in the chair next to me and get comfy. The warm liquid coats my throat, adding to the buzz I started on back at Day's house.

He rests back in his chair. "Let's see." He rubs the scruff on his chin with his thumb and forefinger. *Nice fingers.* "It would have to be in my family's private plane while I was the pilot." He downs his shot.

Slapping my knee, I crack up. "How were you able to accomplish that?"

"Auto pilot, and a very limber partner." He gives me an eyebrow waggle.

"That's impressive!"

"How about you?" He toasts me with another shot.

"A blueberry field. It was scratchy and awkward as we both jockeyed for the top position. My clothes got ruined, and I ended up with a blue butt. I lost the fight for the top, but I made twenty bucks selling a photo of my blueberry stained feet."

He glances at the ceiling, then regains eye contact with a huge smile. "Are you serious?"

"Oh yeah, people pay for feet pics. But that's not the weirdest way I've made buck."

"Really? What else have you done?" He gets up and comes around to the front of the desk to park his fine ass.

I tilt my head back to gaze up at him. His smirk tells it all. "I'll keep the dirty stuff to myself, thank you very much." I bat my eyelashes. "But I was a professional cuddlist. Complete strangers paid me eighty dollars an hour to cuddle with them."

"Why did you stop?" I look at his fine hands folded on his knee.

"It saddened me to come across people who had gone without human contact for long stretches. So, I kept it up for a while until it scored me a stalker. I pulled out as soon as possible and got a restraining order."

"Wait, what about when you dance here? That might happen."

"The bouncers are scary enough to ward off that behavior. But I do take precautions. I never leave here alone and always arrive with someone as well. Rick excels at eliminating weirdos."

"You can rest easy knowing that... I will protect you now that Rick is no longer around. I have big plans for this place."

"Will you remodel the dressing room?" I perk up, leaning forward.

"Rooms. You will each have your own."

"Hey, big spender … what else you gonna do?" I smile.

"An entire renovation. The dance floor, the bathrooms, offices, everything. We'll reach a higher level of sophistication as a club with a membership."

"Sounds great, but what happens to us while you renovate? I'm in a financially challenged relationship with my bank account. I need to get paid."

"All the girls will receive their usual salary." He pats my arm. "And after the grand re-opening … You'll each receive a raise."

"Maybe I can earn enough to get a place of my own and stop sleeping on Day's couch." *Shit, why did I say that out loud?*

"You're homeless?" His eyebrows hit his hairline.

"Um, not really... I've been couch surfing." I play with a loose thread on my top just not to make eye contact anymore.

"I won't stand for one of my girls not having a comfortable bed to sleep in. We'll have to make some arrangements." He rises and goes to his computer.

"No Sir! I don't accept charity... Um, like I mean from strangers." I put my palm up, facing him.

"I'm not a stranger. I'm your boss."

"Still, no thanks." I rise to walk out of the office. His hand on my shoulder stops me cold with a flash of electricity.

"Wait, Gem, I have an idea." I turn. "How about you become the club manager? By making some changes, I can create a fantastic small apartment with a compact kitchen. It's all yours in exchange for being my manager here. We'll continue to pay you your salary for dancing."

"What steps would I need to take to be a manager? I never even finished high school. I'm self-taught at math, science, and history. It was important that I pass my GED, so I studied on my own."

"Sounds like you're an intelligent woman capable of anything I need. It will be just minimal paperwork and keeping the bar stocked."

"I can do that." We shake on it. His hand is strong and warm. I have to overcome this fetish.

"It's a deal." He smiles down at me, and we're close enough to kiss. His eyes are on my lips.

He clears his throat with force and seems to pop out of the moment like someone hit the fire alarm.

All I want is to kiss him endlessly.

BILLY

We walk out to the bar, and the stage lights are on. Music is playing over the speakers as Regina is on stage, giving a show for one. Joe hangs over the edge, money in hand, waiting for her to approach. She is doing a pretty sexy pole dance in a bra top and boy shorts. In no time, her bra hits the floor, leaving her nipples covered with pasties in the shape of stars.

"So, are you a boob man or an ass man?" Gemma sidles alongside me at the bar.

I laugh at her unusual question coming from an employee to her boss. "I guess I'm both."

I can't recall the last time I saw a woman in an intimate setting. Building my empire is taking up all my time.

"I don't believe you!" She turns her body toward me. "All men like both, but they gravitate toward one."

I shrug. "Ok, if you're making me choose, it's the tits. Any guy who's straight has a boob fetish." I push the fresh bowl of peanuts I filled earlier toward her. She takes a huge handful and pops some in her mouth.

"Mmm, salty goodness. I'm starving."

I round to behind the counter, open a bag of chips, and pour them in another bowl. I grab three frozen pizzas from the back freezer, place them in the oven, and set the timer. As I glance behind me, Gem appears with a handful of olives. She pops one in her mouth before talking around it.

"You gonna feed us too? You're a sweetheart of a boss. How am I ever gonna pay you back?"

"No need. I'm just as hungry as you are. Since everyone is drinking, we need something to absorb the alcohol. I take an olive and pop it, mimicking her.

"I love salty. Most people gravitate towards sweets and I like them sometimes. But if I have a choice, it's salt for me." She holds out an olive for me to take with my mouth. When I do, she kisses me on the lips.

I clear my throat. "What was that for?"

"You looked salty, and I needed a taste." She sidesteps me, swinging her hips as she leaves the kitchen.

What the fuck am I gonna do with this one? She's blurring the lines of our owner to employee relationship and it's only my first day here. I'm accustomed to waving off the usual club bimbos looking for a drink. She's so fucking gorgeous no straight guy in his right mind would turn her down.

I stand in shock until the pizza timer goes off. We all eat together at a round table. While we dine, Ray plays softer music. Then I sit down at the piano and start playing a little song I've been writing. When I'm finished, they all applaud and I bow.

"So, you're a musician and an entrepreneur? Let's drink to that!"

We each grab a full shot glass and down it. Joe pours another round. "To just us die hards who came out in the snow tonight."

"Cheers!" everyone says and downs the shot of tequila.

After several more toasts to stuff, I can't even remember … we are all feeling no pain.

"So, how was it?" Gem, intoxicated, slurs her words and speaks louder than a whisper to Ray in her ear.

"He's great!" Ray answers as loud.

"Hey, if you're gonna rate my performance, at least let me hear," Joe says.

"Ok, I give it a nine," Ray says. Bobbing on her barstool like a kid on sugar.

"A fucking nine!" Joe declares as he rises from his chair. "Get over here!" He grabs Ray and picks her up over his shoulder. "I'll show you an eleven. Fuck that, you won't be able to walk when I'm done with you."

Giggling, Ray slaps his ass while making his way to the back room. Gemma smiles as she cleans up the table and throws out the paper plates. I go into the kitchen to wipe it all down and get it ready for an open day tomorrow if the weather breaks.

Gemma is on the stage, wrapped upside down on the pole, when I walk back into the bar. She moves fluidly in her dance, creative in using the metal rod as her partner. The atmosphere is sultry with music playing and dimmed lights. She's wearing a cowgirl costume with a fringe flying around her as she spins. I'm mesmerized by the movements taking a seat to watch. You would never know how strenuous the routine is except for the dew on her skin, making it look luminous.

Gem is gorgeous, that's unmistakable. She's soft and firm in all the right places. Her tits are voluptuous and round compared to her firm stomach and thighs. The way she commands the pole routine is the very reason there's so much definition in her stomach and thigh muscles. Her ass is high and just as beautiful in the shortest jean skirt I've ever seen. When she notices me, her big blue eyes sparkle in my direction. One last spin has her upside down, holding on with just her arms and one leg, while the other leg spreads open to point the toe of her western boot at me. There's just a glimpse of her pretty pink pussy. I lick my lips and watch her dismount. With a simple motion of her index finger, she signals for me to approach and I obey. Her skimpy denim skirt rides up all the way as she kneels on the edge of the platform in front of me. Hands on her tits, kneading them and pushing them together, teasing me. Then she reaches behind and pops the clasp on the bra top to set them free. She surprises me by pulling my head into her cleavage. Her scent surrounds me, intoxicating me more than the four shots I just had. When I pull back, she laughs, leaning back on her haunches and spreading her legs. The eye level view makes me hard in an instant.

Without adjusting my gaze, I warn. "You're playing with fire, little girl."

"This place ain't called The Flame for nothing." She licks her cherry red lips while tracing her fingers down her stomach to her pussy. Moving her thong aside, she rubs her clit.

"That's it!" I grab her bridal style and carry her into my office. I place her on the desk as she's laughing and out of breath.

"You gonna spank me for being a bad girl, boss? Wanna use my fringe as a flogger?" Gemma unzips her arm bands of fringe and slaps me with it. "Take off my boots, please."

I pull off her boots, and she wraps her legs around me, pulling me toward her. She licks her lips. "What ya gonna do now, cowboy? Are you catchin on yet?" She says with a fake southern accent.

"Is that what you want? That show out there was because you want me to fuck you?" She grabs my belt, pulling me in closer between her legs. I watch her expression as she unzips me and discovers what I'm packing.

She sucks air in through her teeth at the sight of my dick. "There's no better way to show a man what I want. A private show is how I roll."

My fist around her throat, I push her down so her back is flat against the old wood desk. It gives me easy access to play with her pussy and ramp up the lubrication. I rip off her thong and she spreads her legs as wide as she can. She's already dripping for me. I discovered a helpful trick to enhance the woman's experience. Using two fingers, I stretch her, getting her ready to accommodate my girth. I love how her eyes roll to the back of her head, how her entire body arches to my touch. She moans at the invasion of my third finger driving into my hand for more. This little Philly ain't afraid to push me.

I fall to my knees, the smell of her arousal all around me. I can't help but taste her. A nibble on her clit has her spasming already. "Billy, please." Her grip on my hair grows intense as her thighs tighten around my face. Pulling me closer, buried as far into her as I could be.

So responsive and willing it fucking turns me on. She can move her hips just like on stage, seeking her pleasure. I dive in and don't let up till she rides out her orgasm. Then, with no hesitation, I stand and plunge into her to the hilt.

"Yes, fuck!" She screams. I take her hard. The desk bumping into the wall with every thrust as she screams for more. It's like an out-of-body experience thinking about how quickly we got here. Nothing will ever be the same.

GEMMA

Present day…

Maria didn't hesitate to find me a position with a wealthy businessman named Benjamin Wixx. She said he picked me himself. I hope I can live up to his expectations. His secretary called to set up an appointment for an interview. The duties he'd require of me are unknown. It's unmistakable. He already has a secretary.

I walk into The Willis Tower with its black metal and wood tone decor. Contemporary design at the finest level. My stiletto heels click along on the marble floors as I find the front desk. A tall, attractive brunette looks up from her computer. She's wearing a designer navy skirt with a pressed white blouse. Silver Tiffany jewelry is on her neck and wrist. *Oh shit, I forgot to wear jewelry.*

My hand reflexively goes to my bare throat.

"I'm here to see Mr. Wixx."

"Name, please."

I clear my throat. "Gemma Bloom."

She arches one eyebrow, holding up her index finger and answering a call on the headphones she's wearing.

"Sorry, did you say Gemma Bloom?" Her snickers are blatant regarding my last name.

"Oh, um I mean Gemma Dedano. Sorry."

"Whew, good. Gemma Bloom sounds like a stripper name, like when you put together a science term and the last thing on your phone pictures." She smiles with her eyes.

"Ha, that's funny. Yeah, my mistake."

It's funny how I'm not one to be intimidated, but that threw me into some serious self-doubt. I glide my palm over my sleek ponytail and assume a more upright position. To think I was toying with the idea of going back to my maiden name. Silly.

"Please sign in here, Ms. Dedano. Take the first elevator on the right. It's the exclusive elevator for Wixx Capital Investment. The car is direct to the eighty-ninth floor."

The elevator whisks me upwards, defying gravity at an incredible velocity. My reflection in the glass shows an acceptable black skirt and white blouse. Simple makeup and sleek hair to convey professionalism. But I didn't have time to get new sensible shoes. I hope these don't scream stripper as soon as he sees me.

Mirrored doors slide open, and I'm in another large lobby area surrounded by windows. The skyline of Chicago is winking at me from the sunlight reflecting off of the tall buildings. The minimal walls are again steel, wood grain, and floors are white sandstone. Another attractive woman in a grey suit, holding a clipboard, meets me at the entrance.

"Ms. Dedano, please come in. Mr. Wixx is on a brief call and will see you afterward. Follow me. Can I bring you something? Water, coffee, tea, soda?"

"Water would be great, thank you." I grin.

"Of course. Please wait here. Make yourself comfortable." She waves me to the seating area.

I sink into a plush leather sofa and place my bag on the floor next to me. My back straightens, legs together, feet flat on the floor. One thing I can always convey is my body strength by how I carry myself. Taking pride in being muscular and fit is important to me. Maybe my lack of education won't overshadow it. This is my first ever formal job interview. I'm used to interviewing by taking my clothes off on stage.

The uncertainty is vexing, and my nerves resurface, making me want to run. Why am I feeling like this? I met wealthy men by the dozen at Innamorare. Except now they will judge my brains instead of my body. Big breath, exhale. Repeat.

The grey suited girl returns with my water not a moment too soon. All this worry has me parched.

"Thank you." I take a sip, then another.

"Of course. I'll be right at my desk if you need anything." She gestures to an area behind a sandstone half wall. Then she turns to leave, stops mid step, twirls around holding her finger up at me. "Yes, Mr. Wixx, sir. "

"Mr. Wixx is waiting in his office for you now. Come with me."

I gulp the water I was sipping, put the glass on the side table and stand. A little shaky on my stilettos causes an inward curse at my weakness. Gathering my bag from the floor, I struggle to catch up.

When she opens the heavy mahogany door and waves me in, she does a literal bow to him before leaving. What the fuck?

The door closing behind me makes me jump. Why am I sweaty? The sunlight glaring behind him is preventing me from seeing his finer features as he extends his hand.

"Ms. Dedano." As I look down, I notice his slender, long-fingered hand. I'm into hands and this one is cold and damp. "I'm Benjamin Wixx. Pleasure to meet you." We shake.

He wears a striking three-piece suit with a gorgeous silk tie. His clothes are the epitome of perfection, custom fit to his athletic looking body. He appears to be in shape, but it's hard to know what's beneath the suit. I'm guessing he's about forty-five years old. At least fifteen years my senior.

"Sorry about the glare. All the better for me to see you, my dear." He presses a button, and the glass becomes shaded, blocking the glare of the sun. Now his well-defined features come into focus. His hair and beard are well groomed within a millimeter, as are his brows. His smile is charming and puts me at ease until I meet his intense eyes. *OK, maybe this* ***is*** *more like my previous interviews…*

Eight

GEMMA

Why do I feel like little red riding hood in the wolf's den all of a sudden? Mr. Wixx is charismatic and polite as his eyes roam my body. I'm accustomed to men wanting me and showing it in their actions. For the first time in my life, though, this is supposed to be a legitimate career. He stands behind the chair, waiting for me to sit. Him lingering behind me causes me discomfort. I turn my head in an awkward position to face him and he walks around to the massive brown leather chair to sit.

His office is enormous. Makes me think he's overcompensating for something. Everything is black, white, and wood tones. The only color comes from the modern art on the walls.

"Ms. Capisi said you have many talents. She confirmed you worked for her for almost two years." He smirks.

He knows I was an escort.

"Um, yes, that's true."

"I think you'll be perfect for the position." He plays with his gold-plated pen, flipping it between his fingers.

"May I ask what role I'm interviewing for? Maria…" I clear my throat. "I mean, Ms. Capisi didn't elaborate."

"That's because I wasn't yet sure myself until you walked through that door, Ms. Dedano. The position is for my personal assistant, involving tasks you may already know and others you may not."

"So, you're saying I already have the job?" I squeeze the armrest with my fingers.

"You had the position when Ms. Capisi called and identified you." He grins.

"I don't understand?"

"No worries. We will get along like bees and honey." He sits up and hands me a list of duties. "Here's a detailed breakdown of your responsibilities and tasks. There will be an expectation for you to conform to the changes sometimes needed to maintain my lifestyle. To be a team player and take action to accomplish what's necessary."

I scan the extensive list, shocked he has me accompanying him to all of his social engagements as his date. "I've always been a team player, sir. But how is it you expect me to attend social engagements with you? Wouldn't that be for your girlfriend or wife?"

"No such thing. No time or desire for relationships. But my colleagues have significant others and I want to insinuate myself into their good graces as much as possible. Having a beautiful woman on my arm who knows how to act at wealthy social events is my ace in the hole for gaining trust. Your salary will be comparable with the upper levels in the company to compensate for the extra face time."

"It gains their trust, making them have the inclination to invest with you?" I nod.

"Exactly!" He taps his finger to his temple. "You'll need an entire new wardrobe which Ms. Grant, my business assistant, will accompany you to the shop. All paid for and with my complements."

Shit, another billionaire throwing money at me. I can't escape from it.

I straighten my spine. "Sir, no need to be extravagant … I can…"

He raises his hand. "Yes, there is! I must have the best dressed and most beautiful woman on my arm. No debate Ms. Dedano. Consider it a requirement of the job."

"Yes, sir." I fold my hands in my lap.

"Oh, and I just want to make sure your relationship with Billy Dedano ended with your divorce. Correct?" He points the pen at me.

"Yes, we are not involved, sir." *Weird he'd ask something so sensitive. I guess personal assistant means many things.*

"Good. Be at my home tomorrow morning at eight o'clock sharp. One of your duties is to manage the staff in my personal residence. Ms. Grant will also train you for that role. She is doing double duties right now and can't wait to have you taking over."

"Yes, sir."

He rises from his seat and gestures to the door. I'm thinking the meeting is over, so I rise, grab my bag, and head to the door. He's right behind me, hand on the doorknob, the other on my back.

"Time for lunch, Ms. Dedano. We are due at Kindling in the next five minutes."

"You mean we're having lunch together?"

"How better to become familiar with each other?"

We take the elevator to the restaurant where he has had the entire outdoor terrace cleared of patrons for our privacy. It reminds me of the night Billy celebrated my birthday for the first time. He rented out my favorite eatery so we could be alone. I must look melancholy because Wixx notices.

“Are you all right? Does this restaurant not meet with your approval? Are you Vegan? I can have them whip up anything you desire, Ms. Dedano.” He motions for the waiter. “May I use your first name since we’ll spend so much time together?”

I grin and, nodding twice, take a sip of my water.

“What would you like to eat for lunch, Gemma?”

Scanning the menu, I pick a salad. He orders a steak with all the fixings. They bring him his favorite hibiscus iced tea with no order necessary. I get the same. When he leans back in his chair, his intense gaze on me, I can’t help squirm a little in my seat. I wish he’d stop doing that.

“Ask me anything,” he says with a grin. “It’s imperative we learn everything about each other.”

“I wasn’t aware it would be required to bare my soul to my boss today.” I shift in my chair.

He laughs. “I employ over forty-two thousand people, Gemma. Rest-assured, I am well-informed about most of them. They all go through rigorous steps before getting a job here. However, I don’t have a necessity to familiarize myself with any of my other employees as much as I need to know you. If that puts you in an uncomfortable position, we can part ways and I will hire someone else. It’s that simple.”

“No, I’m fine with your request.” I play with the drops of condensation on the glass. “How do you spend your leisure hours? What relaxes you?”

He smiles with straight white teeth. It adds to his appeal. “I have various physical recreational activities I enjoy. Some more demanding than others.” He holds my gaze, impassive and confident. My pulse quickens. Then he snaps out of it and lists various interests. “Climbing the Himalayan mountains, sailing, or yachting, golf, various travel experiences. Private safaris, relaxing in exclusive island retreats, and even Arctic expeditions."

"That's an extensive list … Ben? Um, I mean … Benjamin? What is your preference?"

"My family call me Ben, my friends, and business acquaintances call me Benjamin. Which do you prefer to call me? Although you don't seem comfortable with either." His mouth quirks up. He stares appraisingly at me.

"I'll try Ben for now." I fidget in my seat. "What's your secret to being a successful investor?"

"I love money, always have. It's what I strived to conquer and I've succeeded." His lip curls in a wry smile. "Next question."

"Are there any philanthropic causes you support?"

"My philanthropic act is the making of my fortune and helping investors do the same. There's no need to give funds away." He sips his tea.

This guy is an asshole. Perhaps he shouldn't be sitting in a position of great societal power.

"Is money the utmost importance in your eyes? What about health? Love? Family?" I smooth my hand over my skirt.

"Let me tell you a story … There's a billionaire with cancer living in his mansion, having the best doctors in the world taking care of him. He has everything at his fingertips while suffering his illness." He smiles, but the smile doesn't touch his eyes. "Simultaneously, there's another man, same age, same cancer. Without running water or ample food, he calls a tent by the road his home. Both men die of cancer. Which one would you rather be?"

"Have you had to sacrifice any of those things for your work? What about your family?" My finger traces the condensation on my glass.

"My mother raised me and my two sisters. I have no interest in extending my family beyond that."

"What about your legacy? Who will you leave all this to?" I force myself to look him in the eyes for that question.

"I don't know. Maybe after we spend some quality time together, it will be you?" He raises his eyebrows, a cool gleam in his eyes.

The waiter brings our lunch just in time for me to recover from my flustered state. If I had to meet someone with the exact opposite views as me, he would be it. I cannot let myself get further into these kinds of conversations with him. Change of subject, now!

Nine

GEMMA

As we eat, he meticulously cuts his steak into symmetrical pieces before eating them. The potato and green beans are the same. My major focus is not spilling something down my boobs. It's my terrible eating flaw. We fall into a semi comfortable lull in the conversation until they collect our plates.

"My turn, Gemma." He relaxes back in his chair, cocks his head to one side, his dark eyes appraising me. "Tell me about your family."

"That's not a question." I grin.

He smirks. "I can see you're going to add some fire to my days. Do you have siblings?"

Thank God my mom gave birth to no more children after me. Poor souls don't deserve a mother like her. As a child, my fate was burned into history the second I was born in the bathtub of a rat-infested apartment. My maternal figure was a whore who sold herself to sustain her drug habit. She thought she could keep me and raise me, but by the age of five, I was in the mother role and she was the child. Thank goodness my wonderful God-fearing grandmother saved me. When she died, I became invisible to the world.

"No siblings." I sip my tea.

"Parents?"

"Have no idea who my father is … I could be half Scandinavian." I shrug. "Although it's more likely, I'm half bartender or drug dealer who demanded my mother pay her tab."

He laughs at my candor, and it suits him when he laughs. "I appreciate a woman with a self-aware sense of humor. How did you end up walking down the aisle with Billy Dedano?"

"Billy bought the club I was dancing at when I was eighteen. He saved me from the streets … I guess. I was staying at my friend's place, couch surfing, until her husband reached his breaking point. He blew up at my feet resting on the coffee table." I shrug with a grin. "Manners weren't my thing yet."

I sit back and cross my legs. Wixx approves. The outdoor dining space is peaceful since we have it all to ourselves. The sun is warm, or is it him making me warm? It's been so long since I've slept with someone. I must be super horny to be attracted to him. Sure, I had older men paying me to be their companion at Innamorare, but I didn't find them attractive. Could it be I'm just lonely?

"After your divorce, you worked only for Maria Capisi at Innamorare?"

"Yes." I wonder if he knows I went back to stripping? I'm not telling. I adjust in my chair.

"Did you spend the night with the clients there?" His eyes are alight with curiosity.

"I don't think that's anyone's business but my own." I bat my eyelashes at him.

"Ahh, an answer in itself. Do you wonder why I picked you for this job?"

"I don't know, Ben. Could it be that you wish to sleep with me?" I smirk.

This time his smile is a full-on laugh. "I repeat, your candor is intoxicating." He rises, his palm at the small of my back all the way through the restaurant.

He continues in the private elevator. "I picked you because of your past as an escort and as Billy Dedano's wife. You are a beautiful woman who can adapt to any situation, having experienced both poverty and wealth. During your marriage and as an escort, you attended the most lavish affairs. Correct?" I nod. "There, they educated you on how to play the game." A gleam in his eye, he presses the button for the floor of his office.

"Excuse me? The game?" My eyebrows scrunch. The floors fly by on the monitor as we descend.

"Yes, the game." He presses the stop button. "I bet you're an expert." He smiles all white teeth, but his eyes are full of desire.

"How do you mean?" *Is it hot in here?*

"I will give you a scenario and you decide how you would react if I were a client." His voice turns warm and husky.

"Okay…" for some reason, my heart is pounding at a frantic tempo. *Why's he having this effect on me?* This scenario has been my experience with billionaire clients several times. I knew just what task I needed to complete, making them happy and so they'd leave a sizable tip. Taking a deep breath, I put on my professional I've-handled-this many-times facade. *He's no different.*

"I'm your billionaire client vetted by Maria Capisi in all the ways Innamorare demands. We've just had a delectable dinner at an expensive restaurant where you drank your usual amount of wine to be relaxed but not inebriated." He moves closer to me, never leaving eye contact. "I cage you in against the elevator wall like this." He presses my back against the mirrored wall. "Then I sniff the scent in your hair and down your neck. You know what I want. What's your response?"

He smells amazing. I need to keep it together and do the usual. "Are you trying to sleep with me, Wixx?" *Ooh, I enjoy calling him that.*

"Maybe I am." His breath is hot on my neck.

"You're very driven, charismatic and sexy … But I won't sleep with you tonight, Wixx. Sorry."

Just like I would with a client, I place my hand on his cheek and tilt my head as if to let him down easy. Putting his hand over mine, he smiles again and backs away, not relinquishing his hold right away.

"Perfect. An expert at the game. You know how to manipulate while getting what you want. And not angering the other person when they don't. The fundamental key to unlock the riches from the rich."

"I don't get it." I bite my lip.

"You don't have to right now. But you'll be magnificent, my dear." He raises my hand to kiss the back of it. *I'm glad I passed his test. What are his future expectations of me?*

He pokes the button, and the elevator comes to life once again. When we get to his floor, he leaves me with a grey-suited girl. She gives me the address of his private residence and the contact information for Roberta Grant, his primary assistant.

Ten

BILLY

Present Day…

While driving to Ice, I always spot the dark building opposite it. Benjamin Wixx believed it could ruin my business. Fucker lost his shirt in that club and the one he pitted against Flame. He managed to stay open almost a year before shutting them down. I warned him he wouldn't be able to compete with my machine.

"Hey, Billy." I throw my keys to the valet, so he parks my Rolls right in front of the doors and ropes it off to keep hands off. Sometimes I think it's my best advertisement. It brings class and sophistication to the place. Tonight, non-members are welcome to attend our open house, explore our club, and join as members. People are packing the place, and a line is forming around the corner.

"What time you coming tonight? Are you bringing anyone?" I shout into the phone over the music when Joe calls me.

"Fucking go into your office so I can hear without music pounding," Joe says.

I sprint up the stairs to my office overlooking the entire venue and slam the door behind me. The walls are sound proof for this exact reason.

"Okay, what's up?"

"I talked to Ian today. He said Eve's hospital had a benefit ball for the kids' wing and Gemma was there with Benjamin Wixx! Did you do anything yet? Like I told you?"

"Fuck me, he's trying to get back at me. Shutting his clubs down, among other things in our history, transformed him into a rabid fucking dog, and I'm the bone. He discovered my greatest desire and is tempting her away."

"She's still your fucking wife! Go talk to her tonight." I rub the back of my neck while staring out at the crowd in the VIP section.

Then I see her with Wixx.

In my club.

Drinking my liquor.

Enjoying my music.

Joe finishes his sentence. I pound my fist on the desk. Gemma looks hot in top-notch designer clothes. The same clothes hanging in our closet that she left behind. What the fuck is she thinking?

"Joe, I'll see ya later." I hang up, hearing him continue talking on the other end.

As I watch for a few seconds, she's laughing with him. They're sharing a fucking bottle of bubbly. I should be the one she's with. Making her laugh, buying her champagne. Jealousy slithers through my veins, potent and savage in its pursuit to want to claim her as mine again. My head about to explode, I rush out the door and straight to their table. Wixx sees me first, leaning back in his chair with a massive grin on his face. This prick thinks he's won. He doesn't know who he's goddamn fucking with. Gemma sees his attention waver from her to me and turns in her chair. She must read my expression because a hard, obvious swallow gives her away.

"Billy, I'd like to introduce…"

"Get up, come with me. I need to speak to you alone."

"Mr. Dedano, is that the way you speak to your customers? Gemma is enjoying herself and you are ruining her night. I suggest you contact her through your divorce lawyer."

I wanna ring this guy's neck. Gemma stands and puts both palms on my chest. "Please, Billy, let's not make a scene. It won't be good for business."

I growl, staring into her eyes. "Now."

She puts on a fake smile and turns to Wixx. "I'll be right back, Ben."

During the short walk, I calm myself. Here's the thing with Gemma — she doesn't handle her emotions well. Meltdowns happen whenever she feels out of control or exposed. We have her fucked up childhood to thank for that. Before she addressed her alcoholism two years ago, she would drink. Now, I'm not sure what will happen if I push the wrong buttons.

She is pushing my buttons at the moment. As I follow her to my office, I can see right down the back of her dress. I rub my forehead and then adjust my jeans. She already has me aroused.

"I saw you got your Rolls … Congrats, was it worth losing me?"

I lock the door behind me while raking my eyes over her body. "Are you fucking that asshole? You should be careful. There's an agenda."

"Calm down, Billy. I'm not fucking him. I'm working for him." She tsks. "Your advice on the men I spend time with is unnecessary now that we're not married anymore."

She hops her fine ass up onto my desk and crosses those luscious legs, causing her dress to ride up. She picks up my letter opener and traces her fingers with it.

"That fuckface has attempted to seek revenge on my father and me for years. Now, he's using you to do it. He's found my Achilles and is going for it."

"As usual, you think everything is all about you and your clubs." She shakes her head.

"That's not true. You continue to be the utmost important aspect of my life."

She screws up her face at my comment. I can't help myself taking in the woman before me. Her lithe body, smooth skin, and the way her stiletto heels make her calves so sexy. She morphs from disbelief into a frown. "What?"

I find it hard to hold back now as her cheeks pinken under my scrutiny. She knows me better than anyone else and, with little effort, can anticipate my thoughts.

I lean in close enough to have my lips against her ear. "Are you strong enough to walk away unscathed when you realize he's manipulating you to reach me?"

She grabs my collar with her fingers. "What if I'm using him to get to you?"

A challenge for a challenge. That comment has the power to gut me right there. Was she trying to make me jealous?

I grab her ponytail, pulling her chin up so I could obtain better access to her throat. She wraps her legs around me, pulling me in. Nothing says she still wants me more than that. I unhook the clasp behind her neck, letting the dress fall to her waist. Her chest rises and falls with the fever between us. When I slide my tongue over her taught nipple, she shudders. Her hands are in my hair, pulling and wrapping her fingers in the strands while she moans my name.

I back up, taking her in, then holding her gaze, I shove her dress up her thighs. We're like two magnets, always grabbing onto each other.

Black lace panties … she knows they're my favorite. I push the lace aside and find her drenched for me. Her whole-body arches at my fingers, filling her up. So responsive, so willing, she climaxes just from that.

"Get ready for another, my Gem."

I get on my knees. The familiar scent of my wife all around me has me hard as a rod. Intoxicated by her essence, I bring her to orgasm again, twice. She needs to remember how it was between us. How it can be again.

She vibrates with lust in her eyes as I unbutton my pants. Her voice is a whisper when she speaks. "It's been so long. I miss this…" Without a pause, she takes me into her hands, stroking me while sliding off the desk to her knees. She licks the entire length before opening wide and sucking me in. I narrowly prevent myself from falling backward at the sensation of her tight throat.

"Fuck, Gem, I needed this." She stares up at me, but continues to take me deep, over and over. She knows me so well because at the exact second I'm about to lose it, she pops her mouth off. Then she swipes the entire contents of my desktop on the floor and lies back on it, spreading her legs.

Eleven

GEMMA

Lying back on the desk, all I can think about is my intense longing for him. How much I need this. "Fuck me, Billy. Imagine I belong to you."

White sultry heat pulses through his pupils as he stands there, all fucking confident with his dick out. His hands clench at his sides, upper body rising and falling. Anger and lust are warring within him. I know him well, but the result may be unpredictable. He could swear, zip up his pants, and leave. Or he will fuck me raw.

I couldn't help pushing his buttons with my statement. All this feels so natural, so real. It feels like we are united right here, right now. Still together with no issues between us. Playing pretend is fleeting, and when this is over, I'll be thrust back into reality. A life where we're apart. Where his goals and dreams aren't about me. They're about money and power. My heart breaks as my body continues to crave more. Hell, even a hate fuck with him is glorious.

"You'll always be mine! You're my Gem, my wife. Your body knows who you're with. This fucking slick pussy can't lie. If I have to fuck you into acceptance, I will." He grabs my ankles, pulling me to the edge of the desk, penetrating me to the hilt. Such sweet pleasure and pain waft over me. Tears run down my temples and over my ears as my body responds to the explosion inside of me. His heat feels like home, his scent like an aphrodisiac when he pulls me up into his arms. My breasts against his warm chest, my face in his neck. His grip on me is so tight I may break.

The secret is, in my heart of hearts, I already let go of the bitterness, the hurt, and the pain. My longing for him remains. Granting myself with this taste of him is necessary to keep me from running back and begging for our marriage again. If I allowed myself to succumb to that weakness, all my despair in leaving him would have been in vain. Since then I've come so far in working on myself. Until he sees that and me as his top priority, I cannot return. The words coming out of his mouth are the ones I long to hear. But actions speak louder than words. Just the fact that he has that ridiculously expensive Rolls Royce outside proves it.

"Funny how you're always throwing me out on my ass. But tonight, you're fucking me and telling me I still belong to you. This is about control, nothing more." He straightens with me locked in his arms. "You can't have me, but you don't want anyone else to have me, either. Jealousy fuck is what this was and I'll call it as I see it."

"Gemma, that's not true. I've been trying to think of ways to bring you back since the car incident. Baby, we belong together. Come home, we've been apart for long enough."

"I love how you think you can pound your chest and declare I should forgive and forget." I push him off, putting my dress back on. "Thanks for the orgasms. I needed a good fuck. Yet, understand, that was the only intention."

"You're a damn liar. You don't mean a word of that. Remember, just as much as you know me, I know you. What happened here proves your continued love for me. Your desire for me remains insatiable. You've been acting out the entire time we have been apart.

There's no way you can tell me that all that wasn't to get my attention."

"I won't deny I wanted you to wake up and fight for me. You never did. So, I picked myself up off the curb you had fun dropping me on and cleaned up my act. I stopped hoping for you to do something to help me … I made myself move on. The last time I fucked up your cars was when I drew a line in the sand."

"Come on, Gem, you think you can convince me you've moved on? After what we just did? How you respond to me, our perfect compatibility?"

"You assume that because you can still turn me on and give me multiple orgasms that I'm still in love with you?" He stands tall now, tucked in and just shirtless. That smirk and that goddamn muscular chest staring at me. "Sue me for wanting release in a way where it feels like home. But love isn't enough in our relationship. If and when you realize that, is your problem."

I attempt to leave, but he's quicker than I am, grips my hips and pins me against the door. In a tight voice, he says, "I'm not letting you go this time. Fuck! Why are you always leaving me, Gemma? I need us to work this out. What do you need besides my love? I promise to pay attention to you. I'll give you anything you desire. Just come home."

"Words mean nothing to me. I have to leave. Ben is waiting."

He tightens his grip. "You never answered me. Are you fucking him? Because I can't have that. I'll kill him first." His voice is empty, and I've known this man long enough to understand he doesn't mean what he says. He's in defense mode. His anger is floating to the surface, supported by jealousy. He's never even tried to speak to me when I showed up at his club. I was often drunk, and he'd kick me out for causing a scene. Since I cleaned up my act and stopped the craziness, I only regressed one time. A few weeks ago, I entered his garage and vandalized the so-called collector items he treasures.

"I'm his assistant and nothing else. I've worked for him for all of three weeks. Don't get all possessive of me now. We're divorced. Remember?" With that, he lets me go. Those eyes have always been the window to what he's feeling. I can tell there's defeat in them. *It pains my soul to talk to him this way, but I must wait until he can be the husband I need.* I close the office door behind me and lean against it. *If that day ever comes, I'll be the happiest woman on the planet.*

Twelve

BILLY

Gemma's words cut me in half last night. I almost told her we're not divorced until she spoke using those words to me. Saying that she's not still in love with me almost knocked me over. There's no chance she meant that after the manner we connected. Or did she? Gemma could always put sex and love into separate compartments inside her brain. Hell, before I convinced her I wanted a genuine relationship, she was happy with just hooking up every evening. What woman has that kind of thinking? I always thought that after I convinced her about my love for her, that she changed. Maybe she's regressed back to the Gemma she was before we met?

I tend to be the most positive person in the room and avoid negative thinking. But doubts are clouding my mind. I must get her back. Letting her go was the mistake that could define my entire life.

Joe brings over the plans we intend to submit to the Illinois Gaming Board for a state-of-the-art casino, hotel, and spa right on the shore of

Lake Michigan. Two other entities are competing for the last license. The kicker is that Wixx is trying to snatch the license from me.

"What's the damages? Has he bribed any of the board members yet?" I spread open the plans on my desk to take a look.

"I don't know. We may never know. Politics is dirty and money rules the game."

"Yeah, but I'll be a fuckin monkey's uncle before I bribe a politician to get what I want. Fuck em."

"The land on Lake Michigan's shores is fucking valuable. Anything you choose to put there could yield substantial returns. Even just selling it outright as is."

"I'm not backing down easy, man. Wixx is gonna have to pull out all the stops to beat me. I intend to make it miserable for him."

"Don't let any animosity show tomorrow at the hearing. We need to look better. We shouldn't allow ourselves to be dragged down to his level."

"I'll be chill as Lake Shore Drive in the winter." I laugh.

"Why are you in such a good mood today? Did you talk to Gemma?"

I smirk. "It was superior to verbal communication." I lean on my desk and cross my ankles.

"I'm glad you told her."

"I didn't tell her."

"What the fuck, man? Why not?" He pushes my shoulder and I catch myself.

"Like I said, there was no talking. I followed up with flowers. But she hasn't called to thank me. It's not like her."

"You call her! I'm leaving. Call her now."

The cleaning staff is almost finished, and the bar is ready for tonight. I pick up my phone and dial getting voicemail. What is she doing? In the past, she'd never have ignored my calls. I lean back in my chair, gazing out at the empty club.

Gemma Bloom eleven years ago … A country girl at heart. She was a spitfire, seducing me the first night I took over The Flame. We never were apart after that; we'd fuck until the sun rose. I'd drive her home to her friend's house on my motorcycle. Then she'd kick me out so she could sleep all morning. Our club life is chaotic. We're up all night and sleep all day. Once the renovations were done, I helped her move her few possessions into the cozy space I designed on the property.

She surpassed what I'd expected of her as a manager. A commanding presence, she treated employees with respect. All the liquor purveyors loved her. I even got some big discounts because of her charms. It freed me up to pursue other ventures. But you can bet I was back at the club for closing and our time in bed together. No woman will ever compare to her in my eyes. The way she'd strip down and moan my name. Her happiness gave me the freedom to work as I pleased. Then I went and asked her to marry me. Things changed. Her expectations changed. I made the mistake of thinking that showering her with gifts and a mansion would guarantee her happiness with me.

My phone rings, shaking out of my thoughts. Joe sounds upset. "You had to put it out there. Wixx is ahead in the council votes. We have to figure out who we can turn in our direction."

"What about Fahey? I helped him out last year with his directive on the community center."

"He's in our camp, so are Gentry and Copa. We have to sway Peterson or Daniels. I'm still not sure that's gonna do it. He might've gone to the frigging mayor."

"This fucking town, the corruption, just slays me. They're letting this beautiful city go to shit. People are moving out of Illinois in droves."

"Come on, Billy, you and I, we're the diehard Chicagoans, born and bred. I'll never leave this city. I don't think you will either. We can figure this out. I'll contact Fahey to gauge his influence with Peterson or Daniels."

"Let me know if I gotta start making some phone calls." I rub the back of my neck.

"Will do."

Thirteen

GEMMA

Wixx left the club while I was with Billy last night. It figures he wouldn't wait around for me. Two FBI agents are waiting outside for me when I arrive home.

"Hello, Ms. Dedano. We need to ask you a few questions. Can we come in?" The young one holds out his badge for me to examine it.

"I guess, here have a seat in the kitchen. I'll be right back." Kicking off my shoes, I throw a sweater over the revealing dress I wore to the club.

"We believe Benjamin Wixx is laundering cash through his businesses. He's under investigation for tax evasion and drug smuggling as well. Since you're in the middle of his operations, we need you to cooperate with us to gain more evidence."

"Why would I go against my new boss to help you? I haven't witnessed him engaging in any illegal activities."

"Maybe not yet, Ms. But if you discover anything in your duties as his personal assistant, here's my card." The younger and more good-looking individual of the duo states, "Please reach out to us."

The older agent has a pock-marked face and a bulbous nose. "Just to warn you about your rights. If you decide not to cooperate with us and Mr. Wixx is convicted... We can charge you and your former husband as accomplices."

"My ex and Mr. Wixx are not in business, nor are they friends. Why would you assume they are working together?"

"There have been instances in the past where Wixx might have laundered money through your husband's clubs."

"I will think about this and get back to you." They both leave without a problem their business cards on my kitchen table.

The next morning, as I drive to Wixx's mansion in the affluent suburbs, I never noticed how close it is to ours … I mean Billy's house. Leading you further towards the lake, the driveway is longer and features a gentle curve. Living on Lake Michigan is one thing I miss about my life with Billy.

I'm a mess, my mind in complete confusion. Nothing makes me happy anymore. My heart has been kicked around, battered and bruised my entire life. Why am I such a fucking misfit? Never feeling like I belong or have a purpose. Sometimes it's as if I'm that guy who wears the invisibility cloak, but I'm unable to remove it. It just perpetually clings to me. Underneath it all, though, Billy remains in my soul. I want him; I miss him. Will always love him. Our time on the desk last night reminded me of our first encounter at Flame eleven years ago. If only we could return to our initial dating phase. *I can't let all this mess with the cops harm him.*

Wixx's chauffeur is out in front of the house polishing his cars. As I pull up, he stops and gives me a calculating smile. Then he opens my door and waits for me to exit my car. He does not hide the fact that he's checking me out. I'm used to men appreciating my body, so I ignore his blatant examination while thanking him. As I take in the line of shiny cars, I realize Wixx is as obsessed with luxury vehicles as Billy. When I arrive inside, Wixx is waiting for me at my desk.

"Don't you ever disappear on me again! You abandoned me to be with Dedano, which is unacceptable. Why you don't just let the lawyers communicate for you is beyond me. Is there something still between you?" He rises and gets in my face.

"I'm sorry, Wixx, it won't happen again. We have it all ironed out and there's no need for further communication." I put up my hands, palms out. Then maneuver around him to sit in my chair.

"Good. Billy Dedano thwarted many of my business dealings in the past few years. And his father before that. I consider them the enemy, and if you remain working for me, they're yours, too." He leans on my desk with both hands right in front of me.

"You seriously are ordering me to treat my ex-husband as an enemy? I cannot promise such things. I'm sorry."

"Consider yourself on probation for leaving me last night and this matter as well. I'll be monitoring you. For all I know, he's planted you to spy on me."

I throw down my pen, "Come on Wixx. Billy wouldn't engage in that. Nor would I."

"Let's table this discussion. Get to work!" He storms out of my office, almost knocking over the bronze horse statue on the shelf.

Even for Wixx, this is too much. I didn't realize he's so obsessed with Billy. Maybe Billy was telling the truth. *Is Wixx manipulating me to retaliate against my ex? What should I do about the FBI?*

My answer comes in the form of an email. It's from a high-ranking official at the Illinois Gaming Commission. Wixx must have opened it, as I can hear him yelling at someone on the phone from his closed office.

"I don't care how much it costs! Get it done yesterday!" He must have slammed down the phone several times after in anger. I decide never to mention it.

Before leaving, I ensure the staff cleans the entire house. In the dining room, Benjamin's dinner is being served, and only one person remains to clean the dishes.

"I wish to apologize for my behavior earlier. Let me make it up to you with a meal." He's leaning against the doorjamb wearing an expensive suit that fits him to within a centimeter. His face differs entirely from earlier, brow relaxed and even a smile. "We need to discuss the fundraiser."

"I was just about to leave. You want to have dinner here?"

"Yes, it's waiting for us in the dining room. Please come." He grabs my hand, I drop my bag, and I let him pull me out of my office.

"What are we raising funds for with a ball?"

"Children with Cancer." He cuts his chicken in equal symmetrical pieces. Then he chews each bite with purpose.

"Gee, Wixx, I didn't think you had a heart. But here we are, helping kids." I toast him. He smirks and sips his wine.

Throughout the rest of dinner, we discuss the details regarding the preparations that I will be responsible for during the next two weeks. He also requires a special custom-made gown, for which I will be required to attend to fittings.

Then Wixx rises from his seat to look out over the grounds. He opens the wall-to-wall slider and motions for me to follow him outside. The fireplace is lit and there's more wine on the table. The evening air is crisp coming in from the lake. He takes my glass and goes to fill it. I admire the moon's reflection on the water when he sneaks up behind me. I feel the soft touch of a cashmere blanket being draped across my shoulders. But he stays with his arms around me over the wool fabric. I turn my head and look back at him. "Is this a seduction, Wixx?"

"Would you like it to be? No, don't answer that... We need to be comfortable touching to convince everyone we're a couple." He turns me within the cocoon he created with the blanket before he goes on. "Maybe we should even kiss." He rubs his lips against mine. This is crazy, but I'm going with it to gain his trust. "See, this is nice. Pretty soon we'll be natural together."

"Sure, I guess." I shrug.

"Make no mistake Gemma, whilst we raise funds... we will also achieve financial gains. Investors like to feel good about themselves, so they support the charity, whatever it may be. But, when they attend my charity ball, they also hear from my clients how much interest I am making for them on their money. Hence, new clients ask where do I sign and send the money?"

"Is it half for the kids and half for advertising?"

"Your statement is accurate. You'll be in the thick of it, showing everyone a good time so they'll want to return. You're to be considered my hostess. It's communicating with them as if they were your client at Innamorare. Making them feel superior."

"I can do that."

"Black tie, pull out all the stops."

Fourteen

BILLY

It's time to call it a night and go home to bed. Questions about my next steps fill the drive to our home that Gemma and I shared. Two streets away from pulling into my garage, my headlights center on Gemma's car. She bought an old used Volkswagen Beetle right after she left me. There's no mistaking the red bug with a black top and interior. She'd sometimes call it her ladybug. She's pulling out of a gated drive and sees me just as I see her. I check my rearview and pull over to the side of the road. She pulls up and parks in front of my vehicle.

My arms rest upon the beetle's top as I lean into her window. "Hey Gem, where are you coming from at this hour?"

"It's none of your business, but I was still at work." Her head raises.

"That's where Wixx lives?" I gesture with my chin.

"Yup, I just got done." She traces the stitches on the steering wheel.

"You're driving all the way back to the city?"

"What's wrong with that?" There's a slight slur at the end of her sentence.

"Come home to our house. I'll make some of my famous hot chocolate and we can talk." I pat the door and stand straight.

"I'm tired, Billy." She sighs. "What happened in your office — can't ever again. Not until I'm convinced you'll make the effort." She looks down at her hands.

I run my fingers through my hair and bend, sticking my head back in. "I'm ready to put in the dedication, Gem." I lean in further. "But I can't show you unless I'm allowed to see you. Don't drive back—come with me?"

Her silence makes me nervous until a slight nod of her head gives me the answer. There's no possibility she's forgiven me. The only reason she's coming is because she's had a little too much to drink. She's been more cautious about her drinking in recent days, but any amount of alcohol still means keys in the bowl.

"Good girl, I'll follow you."

As soon as I get in the car, I dial Joe. For some reason, I'm sweating.

"Did someone die? Someone better have kicked the bucket for you to call me at this hour!" I can still hear his television in the background. Joe can't sleep without the TV on.

"No, stupid. I need your help. Through persuasion, I managed to convince Gemma to engage in a conversation with me." I rub my palm over my shadowed chin.

"Good, tell her the truth! Goodbye!"

"Wait! Joe, please talk this out with me."

"Okay, shit." I hear his sheets rustling, as he must be getting up. "Bring me up to speed."

"Well, you're aware we had sex in my office. She was ready, willing, and came twice. Yet, as she left, her indifference returned. Then, like I told you earlier, I sent her flowers, which she never acknowledged. Now, driving home, she's pulling out of a nearby driveway. She works for Wixx in his private residence until three in the morning! And he let her drive all that distance drunk. I persuaded her to return home with me instead. Now I'm following her to our house."

"First, get a grip and dial down your anger about Wixx. You need to take care of damage control. Being jealous of her boss won't cut it."

"It's a more challenging task than it seems. A bitch to control it. Maybe it's worse because he's such an asshole. No, strike that. I'd envy anyone she spends this much time with."

"She needs you to be calm and be the voice of reason. Use this opportunity to approach her in a new way. One. Make it seem as if you approve of her choices. Two. See where her heads at. Ask her what it is you can accomplish to improve things between you. Three. No anger or jealousy."

"When the fuck did you become so knowledgeable about how to handle women?" I crack up.

"It's my subscription to Cosmo — help's understanding the opposite sex from their perspective. It's been in my arsenal for years. Lawyers study. Doesn't matter the textbook. It takes work to be the most desirable bachelor in Chicago." He hangs up without a goodbye. *Shithead.*

Gemma pulls into our driveway, and I open the garage doors waving her in to park. A simple conversation is all we need. My approach will be to improve myself and become a better man in order to win her back. *Piece of cake.*

I reach her door and open it for her. She smirks, her long gorgeous legs stretching to bring her to her feet. "Thank you."

"Come on, how about I make the hot chocolate and we sit on the patio to talk?" I place my hand on her back.

She nods and I follow her, checking her ass out from behind. Gem is the exception; she loves it while most women hate it. She once told me that stripping satisfied the need within her to show off her body. When admired, she felt proud for the first time in her life. Her fucked-up childhood put those ideas in her head. Modesty isn't in Gem's vocabulary. She loves her body and wants the attention she gets for its perfection.

We step out onto the patio and she kicks off her shoes, curling her legs under her on the sofa. I grab her favorite soft blanket and drape it over her. She sighs, leaning her head against the sofa and closing her eyes. She looks good in the comfort of our home. I have to persuade her to come back forever.

"I'll be right back with our drinks."

"Hmm—hmm." She sighs.

While I'm heating the milk on the stove and stirring, I come up with my best idea yet.

She takes her hot chocolate in her hands and blows on it. Those puckered lips do it for me just like before we were apart. A move is necessary, or I will lose everything.

I pick up my guitar from where I left it earlier in the day and start playing. The song is from the band Train called "Marry Me" and I sang it to Gem when I proposed eight years ago. When I finish, she looks up at me and smiles a crooked, inebriated grin.

"Are you liking the new job? Wixx treating you well?"

Her face drops. "Billy, I'm in no mood for your jealousy. I signed on to work whatever hours he needs me. The fact that we were working till the wee hours of the morning shouldn't bother you. Especially since you're a nocturnal person as well."

I can't allow her to become angry. "No, no, I think you're getting a clerical job and quitting the other jobs is a successful choice. You're so intelligent and capable. I know you'll succeed."

"Thanks." She sits up in the seat and smiles. "Wixx treats me just like his other employees—except I'm expected to accompany him to different affairs and be a liaison with the clients. Make them feel comfortable, ya know?"

I sip my chocolate to quell my anger before speaking. "Who better to charm the men he wants to reel in than an intelligent, gorgeous woman?" I get up and walk to the rail, putting down my cup. Gemma puts her cup on the coffee table and comes up next to me.

"Look at us! Talking things out with respect. You're even acknowledging that you understand what I'm doing with Wixx. You haven't even answered a phone call during the entire time we've been here."

"I turned it off." I pivot my body to face her, leaning my hip against the railing. "How can I make things up to you and show you I've changed? This is what I crave." I gesture between us. "I want you back in our house, back in our bed with me. What steps would accomplish that in your eyes?"

"I believe you, that you want to change. But until I witness it—I can't…"

"Listen, I have an idea." I grab both her hands in mine. Come back here for easy access to your job at the Wixx mansion. I want to be with you again, and this opportunity allows me to see you every day and prove my love for you.

"I can't do that!" She turns to look out over the lake. "I would just be here alone waiting for you to come home again. It would be going backwards instead of forward."

I grab her hips and turn her towards me. "Please, Gem, I promise to be a different man than I was before. Look how tonight you were too tired and buzzed to drive home. It won't be an issue if you stay here for a while. Since your job takes up most of your days now—You won't even be here much." *That was a hard statement for me.*

Her big blue pupils travel from my chest up to meet my eyes. Her brain works as she bites her lip. The scent of her perfume drives me wild, being so close to her but unable to have her.

Fifteen

GEMMA

It's overwhelming having Billy so close with his hands on me once more. The wine I consumed earlier was causing me to feel light-headed. He's always known how to control my body. By control, I don't mean he ever forced me or took what was not given to him freely. Believe me, I gave all of me over to him with blissful abandon, offering every part of myself to this man. Sex has never been a problem between us. Ever. In this moment, my panties are wet in anticipation and my belly aches for him to throw me over his shoulder and ravage me.

"Gem?"

"Uh, yeah?"

He smirks. "You have that look. You know, the one that says Billy, take me now. I've been able to read that look since the first time I laid eyes on you. You're thinking about it, just like I was."

"You—you were?" I shake my head as if to clear it. "No. I—I wasn't you perve." I glance away, avoiding his intense glare.

His firm grip on my hips tightens and his arousal is poking me in the stomach, causing me to lose all sense. He grips my chin with his right hand, forcing my eyes to meet his stare. "You're thinking about the other night in my office. How delicious it felt to have my cock inside you, your husband making you climax three times in a row."

"So, what if I think about it? I love sex! You of all people should understand I'm insatiable. But it can't happen again. You'll have to call one of your regulars to get you off tonight." I raise my chin in defiance. "You're not my husband anymore."

"Is that what you believe? You assume I fuck around since you're gone?" His nose grazes my throat. "I don't want anyone else but you. You're all I think about when I pleasure myself. And that's the only pleasure I've taken since you left me. The vows I said to you were biblical for me." He kisses my clavicle, running his tongue upward to my ear. "Why can't it happen? Tell me you don't want me."

"I can't lie. I'll always want you. But you have to remember it's just sex. It's forever fireworks between us, though."

His lips are at the top of my bra as I lean back against the railing for support. "That's because we don't just have sex. We make love." With one little flick, he takes my nipple into his mouth, tongue swirling around it.

"Billy, you know I can't resist—please."

"Please what, baby? Please make you come?" With that, his fingers are down the front of my pants, inside my panties. I can't hide that I'm dripping wet for him. I should push him away, put an end to this. But, when his fingers find their destination, my life depends on that orgasm and I can't stop. I grind on his palm, fingers milking me faster as the tingles take over. My lungs pant for air, and my lips wet as the explosions shatter me.

"That's my girl. Chase that release. I can continue until sunrise. In fact, …"

All in one smooth movement, his fingers are gone and I'm flipped over his shoulder. I let out a little scream. "I still hate you, Billy Dedano, for taking the best years of my life. This will be another hate fuck, nothing more."

He carries me back into the house to the bedroom we shared as a married couple. He places me down on the bed, still a wet noodle from my orgasm, and whips my pants off. I cannot defeat the overwhelming raw desire I have for this man. Fuck.

The lust on his face as he kneels before me is undeniable. I'm about to get my world rocked—again. And again. I place my heels on the bed and spread myself wide for him. There's no turning back now. I just lie back and enjoy.

"Fuck, you're so wet for me, baby. I need all of you tonight."

"Holy shit!" I scream as he dives in and makes me come multiple times in a row. Yup, world rocked.

Waking up in my ex-husband's bed and not remembering much about the previous evening is concerning. At least I'm alone.

After finishing my bathroom routine, I set out to look for Billy. I know precisely where he is... every morning he works out to keep in top physical condition. As I approach, I can hear music coming from the gym. It's an old song that a remake morphed into a faster dance groove. It's been all over social media. I hang outside to watch without him knowing. Fuck, he's so damn hot, so strong. He's fucking doing a hand stand using only one arm. His core, back, and arms are engaged in a flex and looking amazing. Up he pops, spinning down on one palm to the song's beat. Right before the music ends, he jumps back upright. Another song begins, and he grabs his jump rope doing all kinds of tricks to the beat and never missing a step. At heart, his performance desire has never changed. I told him he could have made it in the entertainment industry. It's challenging to divert my attention because I can watch this man all day and be blissful. But it's easier to sneak out of the house instead of interrupting his workout.

The phone rings through the car's speakers as I call Eve.

"Hey, how's the job going? Is he treating you well? Or is he an asshole?"

"He's nothing I can't handle. You know I haven't lost my touch, right?"

"I have full confidence you can handle any man." She giggles. "So, what's up?"

"He wants me to organize a charity ball in honor of the kids in your ward at the hospital."

"That's amazing! Did you influence that decision? Thank you."

"Not really. He's doing it for publicity, not philanthropy. But since the kids will benefit, I'm on board. Can you help with the hospital end of things?"

"No problem, I'll send you the forms and we can do it all together."

"Thanks, Eve."

"How are you doing in other areas?"

"You mean Billy?"

"After our talk, I still believe you should attempt reconciliation with him."

"We've been hanging out some. I'm still not letting him know I'm changing my mind, though. He has showed he wants to get back together and see where it goes. Apologizing for his behavior, he wants to make amends. He says work has lost its meaning without me there with him."

"That's a start! He's right, Ian always says … no matter how much success he gains, it wouldn't mean a thing without us to come home to. Go, get the man and have your happy ending."

"I know. Just trying to keep an open mind and heart. I'll keep you posted."

"OK, good luck, and I'll talk to you tomorrow about the ball prep. Bye!"

I turn the radio up in my car as I drive home to shower and change before I have to be back at the Wixx mansion. I skipped saying goodbye to Billy to avoid answering his moving back in question. Wixx would be furious if he knew about Billy and me. Our moving back in together would likely cause a stroke. At this moment, I have to keep things very separate. Being with Billy could become hazardous if I choose to cooperate with the authorities.

Speak of the devil. The two agents are outside my apartment. I put the car in park and step out as they walk over.

"Ms. Dedano, have you thought about helping us bring about justice?" Agent Frost is the older one. He's more menacing in his efforts to make me cooperate. Agent Cross plays good cop to his bad cop vibe.

"It will be easy. You just have to plant a few listening devices, preferably near his office."

"I don't know. What if I end up being caught? Who knows what Wixx is capable of if he catches me?"

Cross says, "We'll give you some tips on placing the devices so that he won't even be able to detect them if he has cameras."

"Cameras? Oh shit. I'm too afraid to attempt this."

Agent Frost leans in. "We have intel that Mr. Wixx is planning on retaliating against your ex if he gets the last gambling license. You wouldn't let anything to happen to Billy Dedano because you refused to assist us. Would you?"

I love Billy too much not to protect him. "No."

"Then you'll help us?" Cross asks. "We'll guarantee your safety."

The words won't emerge from my mouth and my throat feels like I'm being strangled. I just nod.

"Good girl," Frost says as he opens the trunk of their black sedan.

Cross comes over and offers to carry my bag upstairs to the apartment. "We'll show you the correct way in just a few minutes. Then you can go to work."

Once in my kitchen, Frost takes the stuff and spreads it out over my counter. "Look, this device is so small." I nod. "You just palm it and place it when no one is around."

"There are people everywhere around the mansion. I'm afraid someone will see me." I wring my hands together.

Cross puts his arm on my shoulder. Under different circumstances, he'd be attractive. But I'm too freaked out to let myself notice. "You won't. I promise." He goes over some scenarios, including where I plant the device for the best outcome. After they leave, I text Wixx and say I'll be half an hour late. He's fine with it since I stayed last night. I shower, dress, and mentally prepare for espionage.

Sixteen

BILLY

It's a bummer that Gemma left without telling me. She can be stubborn. Even with my top-notch skills, her mind is hard to change. I have to hold on to the fact that she at least let me make love to her. Her interest in having sex with me remains. I'll work from there to persuade her to return to me.

The same way I begin every day is in my personal gym. I push myself harder than needed during weightlifting and running. The uncertainty of my Gem giving me another chance in our marriage creeps into my wayward thoughts. I'll take sex with her any day. But will she allow herself to fall one more time? I find myself running from the doubt to remove Gemma from my head. I need to get down to business, because today is worth money.

But the way she screamed my name allowed me full access to her body and mind in the moment. In that instant—her splayed across our bed, hair fanned out above her head, pink pussy on display—is on repeat in my head. The feeling of longing I have for her is stronger than ever before. The fact she was so quiet and was gone this morning was not a good sign.

Now, I stand in a scalding hot shower, punishment for all the times I ignored her. For how I let her get away. I will never forgive myself. I never considered being with anyone else during these years. It's just not enough to be faithful, invest the effort.

After drying off, I realize it's best she's gone. This morning, I transform into old Billy and handle my business responsibilities. I'm not one to wear a suit every day. Jeans, tees, or a button-down shirt is my usual go to. Not on this particular day. No, today I put on my armor. The black custom-made garment in the closet with all the usual trimmings. My watch, ring, and a text to my driver put me back into billionaire mogul mode.

The council meets now to decide on which company has proposed the best resource for their only gambling license. No other company may apply in the city of Chicago for the foreseeable future. It all comes down to my company and Wixx industries. In the end, I'm hoping the honest guy wins, and that's me. But we all know the old saying that nice guys finish last. Let's hope that's bullshit and once again I will reign over Benjamin Wixx.

Speaking of which, he's here bright and early with his power suit as well. Smug asshole thinks he can win at this game.

"Stop engaging in hate stares," Joe whispers from behind me as he files into the row of seats I'm sitting in.

"Fuck it, sorry I lost the little control I have over my cool." I pull at my collar.

"Gemma?" His eyebrows raise.

"Yup." I run my fingers through my hair, slicking it back.

The board members file into the chambers and sit in their respective half circle of seats at the front. A call for silence convenes the meeting that will decide whether I win the bid or Wixx.

The board confirms a quorum is valid for the vote.

“Something’s wrong, Gentry didn’t show.” Joe grunts under his breath, rubbing his mouth with his thumb and forefinger.

Our lawyers give their final bids for the decision to turn our respective ways, and they vote.

“Wixx industries win the bid for the license by a solitary ballot. Congratulations Mr. Benjamin Wixx.” The secretary of the council announces.

“Fuck! He bought off Gentry to be a no show. He knew they’d have a quorum and the vote would still count.” Joe shakes his head as he walks out of the row.

As I catch a glimpse of the smug face on Wixx, my blood boils. This isn’t over by a long shot. The behind-the-scenes corruption is outrageous. I’m gonna do all I can to reveal the underhanded ways of Benjamin Wixx if it’s the last thing I do. For too long, he has been getting away with too much.

Seventeen

GEMMA

My hands shake as I punch in the code to enter my office in the Wixx mansion. *Get a grip, Gem.* After hanging my jacket in the closet, I sink into my plush desk chair to practice some breathing exercises. Once a calming ritual before performing, now inadequate for saving my life. To make matters worse, Billy's life is also affected. I haven't forgiven him. He will perform many more hours of penance before I even consider it. But I'll love that man until the day I die. I refuse to live in a world without Billy Dedano.

My thoughts drift back to the simpler days when our love story began. I was responsible for seducing Billy. I saw what I wanted and went after him. So many nights, he rocked my world with my cowboy boots up next to my ears. Half the time we were so eager to fuck, we didn't even fully undress.

Another deep breath, and I recount my favorite memory when Billy first showed me his intimate vulnerability. He aimed to prove he trusted me by letting me manscape him for the first time.

"Do whatever you want, Gem. Groom, explore, feel, just make me come in the end," he said, holding up a razor and rolling it between his thumb and forefinger. I looked up at him from sucking his cock and smiled. He knew I liked exploration and wanted to please me.

Running the cool steel over his sensitive areas evoked sensual pleasure, as his taut skin twitched in response. He got comfortable, placing his hands behind his head and spreading his legs. That gorgeous cock stretched up onto his stomach, already seeking satisfaction. I added some cream, giving him a comprehensive grooming. Billy was no stranger to manscaping since his days as a professional bodybuilder, but I'm sure his pubic region has never been this clean. Using a warm rag, I removed any residual shave cream and resumed pleasing him with my mouth. The skin was silky, and bare. From an aesthetic standpoint—very sexy.

"You're making me so fucking hard, Gem."

I straddled him, not able to wait another second to have him inside me. I slammed down, taking him deep while my head fell back in ecstasy.

"Wow, I hope that daydream is about me from the look on your face," Wixx says, breaking me out of my thoughts. It's like sliding down a black tube from your fond, sexy memory to emerge into the glare of your worst nightmare.

Shocked at the intrusion, I fumble upright in my seat. "I, um—I was doing breathing exercises, that's all."

He grins and comes around the desk to stand right next to me. "I won! This time, I end up on top! Get up! We are celebrating today." He hoists me from my chair and twirls me around.

"What did you win?" I ask, pushing on his chest with both palms.

His forehead creases. "You're pushing me away. After last night, why this one eighty?"

"Of course not. I'm just curious." I soften my body language.

"I got the gambling license we've been working towards, over the other applicants, which will complete my financial holdings once the casino is built."

"A casino? That's exciting!" I try to match his enthusiasm, falling short a little. He either doesn't notice or ignores it.

"Come, let's have some champagne." He rubs his palms together.

Wixx leads the way to the living room bar and pours us each a glass.

"It's early. Can I make mine a mimosa with a splash of orange juice?"

He grins, granting my request, and we toast to his victory.

"The construction will begin next month on the five hundred thousand square foot complex. It will rest alongside the Chicago River within Lake Michigan's access. There will be a hotel, museum, boat tours, eleven restaurants and, of course, the gambling."

"Sounds amazing and expensive. How are you starting construction so soon when you just secured the license?"

"A one point three billion dollars projection for the entire project. But compared to what it will generate and how much cash we can push through, it's priceless. I knew we would win because I put my money on the right horse."

I don't feel comfortable asking anymore questions because he just gave some insight why the Feds are keeping an eye on him. Benjamin Wixx is a handsome, wealthy, charismatic crook! My intentions to help the detectives and keep Billy safe is warranted. I plan on planting the listening devices this afternoon in his office. The challenge is to come up with a reason to be in there. Right now, I change the subject to the preparations for the ball.

"I contacted my friend Dr. Evangelina Pope who runs the Cancer Center at the hospital. She and I are putting our heads together on the plans for doing the best good for the children."

"I know of her. She married Ian Ansaldo— correct?"

"Yes, she kept her maiden name in her work."

"I've been attempting to persuade him to invest for years. He shows no interest. Maybe you can sway her to bring him around. His support would confirm to the others that I'm the best."

All I can do is nod. I would never drag Ian into shady dealings with Wixx. This is getting out of hand. I need to take some drastic measures to access his office this afternoon. A plan is forming, but it's not ideal. Using my feminine assets is easy for me. But I'm not a fan of having to follow through with Wixx.

Eighteen

BILLY

Eight years ago…

The Flame is packed tonight because I open the club to non-membership customers one night a month. It builds interest and attracts more members. We put on a spectacular show and treat everyone as royalty. This is the standard we provide to our members as well for their pricey monthly dues. A year ago, I transformed the place into the upscale spot it is today.

Gemma is dancing to her favorite country song on stage in her red, white, and blue fringed costume. There's shouting about patriotism or something and a guy throws a beer bottle at her. It hits her in the skull and he laughs. I jump out of my seat at the bar and tackle him, murder in my veins. I'm gonna kill this mother fucker with my bare hands. Before the bouncers pull me off, I inflict some damage on the asshole. He's so high he can't feel a thing and tries to fight back the best he can. Only to lose. I call the cops and press charges of assault with a weapon. Death would have been too good. Fuckin' asshole. The professionals they are, my dancers didn't let the altercation ruin my business. Dayo got right up on the stage and continued the show after I carried Gemma out of there.

Gem needs a hospital. Her forehead is bleeding, and she passed out once already. I grab a clean towel to catch the blood. A head wound bleeds like a motherfucker. I'm confident I can transport her to the hospital quicker than an ambulance. She lets me carry her to the car while she holds pressure on the wound. It's lucky the emergency room is almost empty because of the hour. After filling out the forms for her, they take us right away. The ER doc finishes stitching her forehead, then they take her for a CT scan. Afterward, my hope that they go away and leave us alone behind the curtain is granted.

I approach her from all the pacing I've been doing. She smiles when I kiss her hand. "That's your last performance. You don't need to dance anymore because you have a nice apartment and I'm giving you a raise for your management job."

"Come on, Billy. It could happen to any of the girls. I'm fine." She rolls her eyes.

"You're not any of the girls! You're mine. Nobody hurts what's mine." Now she looks at me with wonder. The look tells a story full of unsaid feelings. Fuck, I ask myself why I've become so protective all of a sudden. Gem is all I can think of, and she means everything to me.

"I'm writing a prescription for pain." The doctor interrupts my rant. "You shouldn't be alone for two days. You've sustained a serious concussion," Dr. Green says. He looks at me and continues. "Will you be the one staying with her?"

"Yes, Doc." I nod.

"Good." He points his index finger at me. "Make sure you keep an eye out for any new or worsening symptoms. Such as persistent headache, vomiting, confusion, weakness, numbness, slurred speech, or seizures. The presence of any of these symptoms may indicate a severe injury that requires immediate medical attention." I grab

Gem's hand. "Rest is crucial in the early stages of recovery. This implies physical and cognitive rest."

"I'll make sure she follows the rules." Gemma rolls her eyes at me again.

"No work until the follow-up appointment. The nurse will schedule it after clearing you." Dr. Green hugs his tablet and leaves the room.

While I insist Gemma stay at my house for the duration of her recovery, she's reluctant. She voices her thoughts on the way. "We're not at a place where I should be staying with you. Sometimes, Regina checks on me. I'll be fine. I've been on my own since a very young age. Always have taken care of myself. This situation is no different." She wets her lips and kind of hugs the passenger door.

"What the fuck is that supposed to mean? Every evening for months, we've spent together. In my opinion, that means you can live with me for a few days."

As a guy, I don't relish talking about relationships and where we are in them. But this incident has brought out protective feelings inside me for her. It's undeniable, the urge to look after her. I don't plan to declare my eternal love for her at this moment, but I want to support her. *Wait—love? Am I even entertaining that idea?*

"We've been 'fucking' for months every day. It's been about not being able to keep our hands off each other. Not about a relationship where we're exclusive and heading towards living together." She tilts her head, pressing her lips together.

"We're not exclusive?" *Fuck! I sound like a needy idiot.*

"I thought you'd be with other women since so many hit on you. It's OK, I get it. I'm used to being on my own, alone. Sex is sex, right?" When she rolls her eyes at me again, I decide this is something I need to address in another conversation soon.

No more eye rolling towards me in the future.

"Uh, Gemma, when do you imagine I'm with these women? Be logical. I'm here with you at the club while working and we leave together every night." I squeeze the steering wheel tighter.

"I guess I never thought about it like that." Her eyebrows raise and she winces at the numbness wearing off.

"You're feeling the stitches, I can tell. As soon as I have you settled into bed … pain meds." I put my palm on her leg.

She rests back against the headrest and sighs in defeat. She's coming home with me.

I can't say Gem didn't turn me on, stripping down and throwing my t-shirt on over her naked body. Her presence in my bed for the first time is eye-opening. I want her to stay and never leave. The meds do their thing and she settles in, muttering, "Now what? Are we dating now? I don't date anyone. I just fuck." She sighs, lids already closed almost off to dreamland. "I love sex. I love sex with you." Then she's out.

I crack up at her last statement. It's not unwarranted. I've never taken her on a date. Why would she assume we were more than fuck buddies? It's time I rectify that and get my head out of my ass. Gemma needs to know I care about her and I'm gonna show her. It appears by her statement in the car that she hasn't had someone care about her in a genuine way. The no strings language she used stems from the probable toxicity of the household she grew up in. Regina mentioned to me a small part of Gem's history when she thanked me for giving her friend a comfortable apartment to live in.

I've decided it's the right moment to work my way into her closed off heart and not just her bed. My goal is to reassure her and ease her into the realization that I'm not someone who will let her down.

With my index finger, I push her hair back and admire her beauty. When I lie in the bed next to her, she curls around me. An instinctive gesture. Taking care of myself in the shower after my workout was a smart idea to make sleeping next to her easier. Before I nod off, I plan our first official date.

Nineteen

GEMMA

Billy was the epitome of boyfriend material yesterday. He treated me like I was his family. Never has anyone except my grandmother served me so well. Maybe some of that is my fault, considering after she passed, I built a barrier around my heart and pushed away anyone who showed they cared. What should I do about Billy? Should I gamble and see if this can last? Or should I end things now and protect my walled off ticker? Remember what I said before?

Our choices change the trajectory of events…

Or will fate laugh and bring me full circle face to face with my destiny, anyway?

The crack in the blinds let dawn's light blare at me. This headache feels like my heartbeat is pounding under my scalp. The t-shirt Billy gave me is up around my midsection, leaving me buck naked from the waist down. I kicked off the covers because of the human radiator next to me. Billy's flawless body is there, his steady breathing a calming sound. I seize the opportunity to admire him. Years of dedication sculpted this chiseled physique. Every muscle rippled with definition, a testament to his commitment to the craft of bodybuilding. Countless hours in the gym pushing the limits and striving for perfection. It's evident he's meticulous in attending to every muscle group on a schedule, from bulging biceps to a rock-solid core.

I can't help but touch him, running my fingers over his six-pack. All I can think about is licking him from tip to tip. My dirty mind surfaces even in the path of my excruciating headache. I'm such a nympho sometimes.

"Oh, no you don't … no fair waking me like that when you're not supposed to engage in anything physical." He catches my hand before it slips under the sheet to his groin. "We have to follow doctor's orders—No matter how blue my balls get." With a soft kiss on my palm, he places his palm over mine on his stomach. Eyes pop open, he assesses me. "You too warm?"

"You're like sleeping with a radiator. It will be useful in winter, but this instance I was hot." I blow air out of my lungs through pierced lips.

"Sorry about that, babe. Tonight, I'll turn down the air."

I sit up, feeling dizzy. He rushes to steady me. "I'm OK. Just a little dizzy and a headache." My fingers grasp my forehead.

"Try not to move too fast. Stay put while I get you some aspirin."

Billy does not hide his morning wood as he slips on his boxers. I must admit it's quite impressive and why hide it? If I was feeling better, I'd jump on that.

He returns with a glass of orange juice, some saltines, and two aspirin. "You need a tiny something bland in your stomach to soak up the meds. Eat a few bites of cracker before downing the pills."

I nod and comply with his request while he fluffs the pillows behind me. "What's with the pampering?" I can feel my face screw up.

He smiles. "Can't you just relax and let me take care of you?"

"I don't know. It's kinda weird since we're just into fucking. What's this change in you?"

He sits on the bed and takes my hand. I look from our hands to his pupils. He seems sincere. "Can you accept I want to strengthen this between us?"

"Are you sure you're not the one with the concussed head?" My voice is still kind of gravelly.

He belly laughs and wraps me into his arms. I put my cheek on his shoulder as he strokes my hair. A foreign flutter erupts in my heart, warming it to him. This is the moment he breaks through. I've fallen for Billy Dedano.

This is the first chance I've gotten to Billy's home. His apparent success is unmistakable from the club's renovation and now with his house. The colors are subdued and masculine in hue. Only the most impactful decorative objects grace the rooms with clutter non-existent. I glimpsed only the parts on the way to his bedroom, yet I presume the aesthetic remains consistent throughout.

After lounging in bed together, eating bacon and eggs, Billy walks me to the pristine white marble and glass bathroom, where I'm left alone for a few minutes to pee. Seeing my face in the mirrors, I'm shocked by my black and purple skin.

"Bruising around the eyes is common with your head injury, so don't worry. Arnica to soothe the pain." He uses a cotton swab to apply it on the delicate skin.

Still a little unsteady, he stands nearby while I wash up further and brush my teeth with a brand-new toothbrush he provided. I rinse and he takes a fluffy towel, wiping my lips, before giving me a gentle kiss. He knows how to make me feel special, something I'm unaccustomed to in the past.

The time flies by as we listen to soothing music. I rest as he works out in his gym, then he orders for dinner. The entire day, I never change out of his t-shirt. I can't remember an experience like this ever in my life. Tending to my mom when I was a child and going to work when I was older prevented me from nursing my wounds.

He makes a few phone calls where I overhear the instructions he gives the staff at the club. He can't be absent without me there to hold down the fort. I round the corner into the living room, where he's perched on the sofa. "So, you're staying home to care for me?" Really, that's unnecessary. It won't be good if we're both absent tonight.

"You don't worry your pretty brain. I have everything under control. Come sit next to me."

He pats his lap for me to lie down with my head on it. His smooth fingers caress my temple and run through my hair. He puts me in a trance and I drift asleep right on his lap.

I wake up in Billy's bed, with no memory of how I arrived last night. He is serene beside me, still as gorgeous as yesterday. My strength has increased and I can rise with no problems. It's still early, so I sneak out of bed to take a shower. I close the bathroom door, holding onto the handle not to wake him and turn on the water to warm. Billy's shirt is discarded on the floor as I jump in under the luxurious spray. I shut my eyelids and enjoy the water cascading down my naked body, when powerful arms envelop me.

"It's unbelievable you would assume I would let you out of my sight? What if you become dizzy and fall on the marble?" He rests his chin on top of my head with the lightest touch.

I roll my eyes, turn in his grasp, and look up at him. "I'm OK, Billy. You don't have to be like this. We can go back to just sex. Pick me up and fuck me against the wall." I'm eager for the prospect.

He grabs my chin between his thumb and fingers, almost as if when we played it rough in the past. At first, I think he's gonna grant me my request. He knows it makes me hot when he acts all alpha. "For every time you roll your eyes at me, I'll make sure you face the consequences once you're feeling better."

"Show me now! Let's have shower sex. Show me who's the boss, baby." I stand up to him, straightening my spine.

He laughs wholeheartedly. "I would love to, but I can't. Doctor's instructions say light duty for one more day. Now be a good girl and let me wash you so you don't end up wetting your stitches." Before he lets go of me, he surprises me with a knee buckling kiss.

He cleanses my scalp and the rest of me with the softest of touch. I won't lie. It's sexy and provocative. I'm so turned on by his care. After rinsing me, I notice how hard he is … Not a situation I can ever ignore. "Let me … I want to…"

"We can't, my little nymph. You need to rest." He goes to turn off the shower, but I stop him.

Without averting my gaze from his enormous erection, I suggest, "I'll relax here under the warm water and rest while you perform for me."

"You mean you want to watch me pleasure myself?" he asks, eyebrows raised.

"In my opinion, there's nothing hotter." The cocky smirk tells me he's in. As a professional bodybuilder, Billy shares my love of performing. Our bodies served as performance tools in different venues, yet the desire to entertain unites us. Lucky for me, I get a private presentation.

"As you wish, my beautiful gemstone." He winks.

He lays a towel on the marble to prevent my ass from feeling the coldness. Multiple jets spray us from the walls. With a squirt of soap on his hands, he starts at a leisurely pace. I lick my lips, wanting to participate, but knowing he won't allow it.

The ripples in his taut abs and each glorious inch of flesh below are on display for me to cherish this memory forever. His long black hair wet and slicked back, thick dark eyelashes clumping together as his neck bends back in ecstasy. His ministrations produce the desired effect, causing the muscles in his throat to become corded and strained. The color of his skin flushes, even darker on his cock as it hardens. I spread my legs and my fingers wander to stroke my clit. I can't help myself.

He's on the precipice of his orgasm while I search for mine, spearing two fingers inside of me over and over. I don't dare look away in fear of missing his release. It's glorious. When it comes, I fall over the edge right after him.

We finish rinsing off, and Billy grabs the towel from the warmer to wrap me in. It feels luxurious and soft against my skin. He ties another around his waist and kneels before me to dry my legs.

"What are you doing?" My eyebrows wrinkle.

"No bending over to dry your legs! … Especially since you disobeyed doctor's orders while in the shower. An orgasm makes the blood rush downward out of your head." He bites his lip.

I sigh, letting him have his way. The new Billy is mindboggling. It scares me to accept the feelings surfacing inside me. I don't deserve to take any of his caring or strength. It's easy to become reliant on that. Easy to unload on him the worthlessness and despair. I have nothing to offer him except sex. Our previous arrangement was equal, the giving and receiving of pleasure. We existed on the same level.

Bringing me out of my thoughts, I watch in awe at Billy's male beauty. I lean against the wall, staring. While he dries himself off and applies his deodorant, I feel a surge of desire to claim him as mine. He's devastatingly gorgeous.

"You keep looking at me like that and I'm gonna lose all my control.

Come on. You need some clean clothes to put on. My day will be less challenging once you have all your clothes on."

We eat a breakfast filled with protein required for his strict diet to keep his body looking so impressive.

"I'm heading into the gym. Feel free to explore, mi casa su casa." He kisses me on the forehead, careful not to touch my stitches.

I tie up the big t-shirt he gave me into a knot and roll the waistband of his gym shorts to fit me better. Then I begin my exploration. I've never stayed in a place as nice as Billy's condo. He's building his club empire with a systemic plan while keeping his possessions reigned in. I have to admire how he wants to accomplish it all himself and not depend on his father's or family's money. He needs to prove something, either to his father or himself.

Pictures line the sofa table of his family and friends. Lucky to have so many close loved ones. With Dayo and her husband gone to Nigeria, only Regina remains for me. Sometimes I feel lonely in this big world all by myself. It's the reason I'm tempted to conform to Billy's new idea of a dating relationship. But would that be for selfish reasons? Am I letting myself fall for him out of loneliness?

Another room catches my eye and I explore further. Books in every genre, from business to romance, line the walls. I have a passion for reading and did not know Billy felt the same. This library proves he has a respect for the written word as I have. I consider books a luxury when I can save money for them. I always pick with thought and angst, wanting the book to live up to the sacrifice of the savings.

Running my fingers along the spines, I select a romance and curl up into a chair by the window. Immersion in the story is immediate, reading voraciously to witness the conclusion. I'm a fast reader when I wish to be. I just slow myself down and limit chapters when it's necessary to savior the story until I can afford another book. Maybe Billy will let me borrow some from his collection.

"Hey, I see you found my library." He puts air quotes around the word.

"It's wonderful. I love to read." I gaze up from the words.

"One day, I will have a library lined with walnut wood shelves that run two stories high. I'll fill it with books." He splays his arms above his head.

"That's a glorious dream." I smile.

"Not a dream. I'll make it happen. It will be in an enormous mansion on Lake Michigan with an underground garage to accommodate all my rare automobiles." He holds his palms out in front of him, picturing the garage.

"You're such a driven individual—I believe you'll accomplish anything you put your mind to." I tilt my head, smiling.

"Thanks, hey how about a movie and some popcorn?" He holds out his hand and I grab it.

"OK, I get to choose what we watch." I smirk.

"You're the patient in recovery—so, of course!"

"Magic Mike. It's about time I enjoy a mind-blowing strip tease. Not perform one." I almost skip to the living room.

"I'm happy to oblige anytime you're in the mood and not recovering from a blow to the head."

"Oooh, great idea! Can't wait to see that!"

He grins. "I've been a professional bodybuilder. Performance is key."

"I'm gonna hold you to that offer," I say, wetting my lips.

He gestures for me to sit and places a blanket over me. Then he hands me the remote. "Here, find something you'll like. I have all the channels. I'll make the popcorn."

I find the film and savor the aroma of popped popcorn. He returns with a tray of drinks and popcorn seasonings.

"These are great for flavoring your bowl. I already added melted butter." He offers the tray.

"I choose sweet and salty. I live for the combo."

"Me too." He sidles up next to me, putting one gigantic bowl between us as I press play.

This is so normal compared to what we have done together in the past. I mean, I love fucking this man. But this is also quite remarkable. A guy waiting on me isn't so bad. Being independent doesn't prevent me from enjoying a sexy man without sex.

Why is it when you can't have something you want it more? Like a tall glass of tap water in Mexico. It sounds refreshing, but you'll end up with the shits. Here I am watching a movie with Billy, when all I crave is to have sweaty, naughty sex with him.

Twenty

BILLY

There's an emptiness in my home since Gemma left. She was past the point where the doctors told her she needed observation. It seems all is right with her concussion and the doc released her. I attempted to devise a way to keep her here. We got comfortable with each other. I would never pressure her, but I fuckin miss her here with me.

It's Saturday night, we're going to the hottest restaurant in Chicago on our first official date. She's getting ready in her place adjacent to my club. I fine tune the instructions for my bartenders and wait staff while I wait. When Gem is twenty minutes late, worry sets in. I knock on the locked door of her apartment.

"Gem? We're going to miss our reservation. Are you ready?" I lean against the doorjamb.

She opens the door, a vision in a little blue dress. The color in her eyes pop. Big vibrant blue pupils surrounded by long lashes—and tears. I adjust my posture, angling my neck.

"I'm sorry." She flaps her palms against her hips.

"Hey, why the tears? You look so beautiful. There should be nothing to cry about. We're going on our first official date." My voice is cheery on purpose.

She sniffles and turns to walk back inside. "This is my first official date ever." She grabs a tissue, blotting her eyes. "Men don't date a girl like me! What are we doing? This cannot end well."

I take her hand, and we sit on the sofa facing each other. "Listen, I have no fucking idea what I'm doing with dating, either. All I know is I need to get my head outta my ass and show you how much you mean to me. In the past few months, I've been the jerk that treated you like every other asshole you met. No more!" She looks up at me with pathetic teary eyes and I wipe her cheeks with my thumbs. "Things are going to be different … Now, we'll converse, savor food and wine, and deepen our connections. We'll keep dating until you accept the fact that I'm not leaving you. I will never hurt you. I'll offer protection, respect, and care. Once we begin, it is my hope you will become convinced and feel as special as I know you are."

"You're saying all the words that I thought no one would direct towards me. My brain has accepted the conditioning that I will never have the happy ending. How do I reconcile all this within myself?" Tears stream again as she blubbers through her sentence.

"Don't overthink, simply sense—engage with what I aim to show you." I take her face into my palms and kiss those pouty pink lips to within an inch of our lives. She's breathless.

When we part, she takes a deep breath, then nods. No words. She gets up and, with a determined walk grabs a sweater.

Roister is the hottest restaurant in town, where the kitchen is the restaurant. I pulled some strings to get the exclusive seats. The food is rustic with vibrant flavors. I order oysters as an appetizer to which Gem wrinkles her cute little nose. But she's a trooper and tries one. Even if she hates them, it still provides a new culinary experience for her. My goal is to show her the finer things in life and help her realize she deserves to enjoy them.

"Can we share? I mean, order what we each want but share the entrees?" Her big blue eyes are wide.

"Of course. What are you in the mood for?"

"I have this inclination to order something wild and unfamiliar. But I'm just gonna get the chicken." She grins, licking her lips.

"How about the roasted duck? I think you'll be surprised at how similar the roasted duck tastes to chicken. And It's a little crazy." I smile with all my teeth, making fun. "I'll order the fish and we'll share. If you don't like either, we can order something else."

She shakes her head in a quick back-and-forth movement. "Oh no, I wouldn't dream of wasting food. I love sea bass and I'm sure I'll like the duck as well."

The waiter delivers the food and my girl eats like a champion. The joy in her face just exploring food is addictive. She's not shy about tasting everything on the table. Watching her savor the food is turning me on. I can't wait to give her my surprise later.

We make our way back to the club and meet up with Regina and Joe for a few cocktails. Looks like they're still goin' at it. She's a wild one up on stage and Joe has no qualms about showing his appreciation. As the end beats wind down in her song, the bartender announces the last call. Aflame empties right after.

"Hey, bro, Ray and I are leaving. Thanks for the drinks. We had fun," Joe says.

"See ya, don't do anything I wouldn't do." We both laugh.

"That means sky's the limit, right?" He winks.

"Absofuckinlutely!"

I have a pretty decent buzz going on after the wine at dinner and the shots with Joe. Perfect for my surprise. Gemma and Ray come out of the bathroom and Ray takes Joe's hand to leave. I lock the door after them. When I return, I find Gem cleaning up the empty glasses behind the bar.

"You don't need to do that. You're off tonight."

"I know, just makes me nuts when dirty glasses sit overnight." She shrugs.

"Be right back, office check."

Once in my office, I drop and do some pushups to pump up for my performance. In my competition days as a bodybuilder, the performance was half the score. I'm confident I can pull this off without looking like an idiot. I can't wait to see Gem's face when I channel Channing Tatum's strip tease from the movie as I promised her. A pair of grey sweatpants, a white t-shirt and a hoody with a red baseball cap is already here in my office. I cued up the sultry seductive R&B track earlier today so I wouldn't have to search now. The lights remain seductive, just as Regina left them, and ideal for my dance. I'm hoping Gemma likes it.

Twenty-One

GEMMA

The speakers fill the room with the seductive opening beats to the song Channing Tatum used to seduce women across the planet in Magic Mike. I must say, the enticing R&B track sets the backdrop with its pulsating rhythm. Realizing what's ahead, I let the anticipation and excitement consume me.

I dash out of the bar and snag the front-row seat for what promises to be a captivating treat.

Billy poses in the stage's darkness, the perfect male form, until the music cues his moves. He rolls his neck in a circle, still in the hood of his sweatshirt. Next, unzips it and discards it. He's in a white tank and God help me, grey sweatpants.

He tugs down the brim of his red cap and pumps his hips to the beat. After he loses the shirt, his defined decadence is exposed for my viewing pleasure. My mouth waters along with my nether region at the sight of his chiseled physique. His spins and slides are on point and when the soundtrack crescendos he does the half push up, half hump the floor bit. It drives me just about over the edge. I give a whoop and start grinding to the music as well.

Billy comes over and picks me up onto the stage like I weigh nothing. He puts the red hat on me and continues his dance up close and personal. Taut, tan skin over a firm, muscular underpinning covers his entire body. He runs his fingers through his chin length dark hair as his eyes flash in my direction, devouring me as I am him. The metaphors and innuendos in the words of the song convey the intensity of the attraction between us. His moves are hypnotic, drawing me further under his spell.

I lean my spine against the pole I've performed on many times. I strike a pose with my hands above my head grasping the stainless steel, my tits pushed out into his face. He seizes the opportunity to get up close and personal, sliding his palms downward from mine over my skin, skimming it with his fingers. Giggling, I fan myself before turning and sticking my ass out for him to grind his exceptional bulge. Now we're playing dueling dance moves when I respond with a couple of body rolls and a hair flick. I pull up my mini skirt and invert myself onto the pole, spreading my legs to give him a peek. He's on me before I can dismount, holding my legs apart, dipping his face into my crotch. He knows I'm fit enough to stay inverted for the time he takes to show appreciation for the reveal by pushing aside my thong and giving a swipe with his tongue.

Needless to say, foreplay has reached extra levels of exquisite. When we collapse onto the ground, my hands are in his pants. The moment my touch meets velveteen steel, his stomach ripples with tension, his eyes falling backward. The music ends, leaving only our moans in the club. I savor him, teasing with my tongue and a gentle scrape of my teeth.

"Fuuuck, Gem. That feels amazing."

"I think that performance deserves amazing." I dive back in, pleasuring him with my mouth. His hand falls on my scalp, fingers threading through my tresses, until he reaches his breaking point.

"It feels so fantastic, baby. But hold off, I'll make you feel just as good."

I look up at him as he stands and pulls up the sweats. He reaches down and I grab his hand for help up, slamming into his glorious chest. His palms graze my cheeks and slide into my temples as he kisses me, taking full possession. He cups my ass, pulling me up to straddle his waist, never losing the connection of our mouths.

Somehow, he finds his way to my bed in my apartment while never ending the kissing. My rear presses against the mattress with Billy's weight on top of me. He unbuttons my blouse, drinking in the taste of me as his lips follow his fingers. Large, smooth palms find my breasts as he rolls my hard nipples between his thumb and fingers. He takes his time worshipping me with his lips, his tongue, until he reaches precisely where he wants to be. My skirt still up around my waist, he rips the small strap of my thong panties to hit home.

I whisper, "Oh, Billy," and open wider, inviting his exploration. Then again, I scream it when I shatter into pieces. After stripping us both down to nothing and donning a condom, he brings me back in a slow and languid manner. He makes me ache to have him inside me. "Please," I beg.

With that, he yanks me by my ankles to the end of the bed and penetrates me to the hilt. Glorious waves of light flutter through my mind. Billy makes love to me. I relish the feeling as he sinks inside me. It's as if he's entranced by the sight, the slow push in, the slick pull out. It's so fucking sexy to watch his abs clench as he pushes inside, but I need more … I reach forward and tug his ass toward me, driving him in so deep the air leaves my lungs. I feel so full and the quivering in my womb is sublime.

Billy loses himself in a fiery haze as he speeds up his thrusts. Every corded muscle straining, damp with sweat. His moans as he releases are primal and cleansing. His words from earlier repeat in my brain. *"Don't think, just feel—experience what I want to show you."* A sight and sound I will cherish in my mind, as in that moment I know.—I love him.

Twenty-Two

GEMMA

Present day…

Agent Cross texts me to see if I have a clear window to plant the listening devices and cameras today. The judge signed off with a court order. Now whatever they hear will be admissible in Wixx being indicted. The rest depends on my success in planting them without being seen.

If Benjamin catches me in his office, my plan is to seduce him. My presence has no other known explanation. Except, maybe a feeble attempt to use the file I promised him. In snooping on his calendar, I found he has a dinner meeting with the architect today. It just might be my chance.

Six o'clock rolls around and my palms are sweating. I wash up in my ensuite bathroom in my office and unbutton a few top buttons on my blouse just in case.

Deep cleansing breaths in front of the mirror, and then I grab the folder with all the details of the charity ball. I lock my workplace and walk to the wing where Benjamin lives.

Dusk is fading into night, and the hallway is lit with one dim sconce. His door is closed and the lights are off, signaling to me he's left for the day. With stealth, I check and find it unlocked, signaling that this will be my only chance. So, I tiptoe to the desk where Wixx's computer sits dormant. Pulling the three small devices from my pocket, I begin the delicate task of planting them. One beneath the corner of the desk. One behind a book on the shelf near where I have seen him pace while speaking on the phone. Last, the corner of the Monet picture frame.

The tension in my neck and back is painful as I hear distant footsteps setting my nerves further on edge. I compel myself to remain calm and focused if I have to lie. I'm convinced someone is outside in the corridor.

"Mr. Wixx, are you ready to leave for your meeting?" A man's voice says as he knocks and his hand wiggles the handle.

Benjamin's chauffeur is about to catch me in the act. Should I hide myself or should I act as if I belong there dropping off the files?

Time does not allow for thoughtful decision-making. The door opens, and he sees me. "Hello, Ronald. Mr. Wixx isn't here."

His eyes glaze over at the sight of me in a predatory gaze. "Ms. Dedano, what are you up to in here without Mr. Wixx?"

I smile my flirtiest smile before answering. "Same as you, silly—looking for Wixx." I try to walk past him and he grabs my arm. "What are you doing? Let go of me!"

He spins me, pinning both my arms behind me, then enjoying the view of my tits from where I unbuttoned earlier. His grin is maniacal as he boldly sniffs me. "How about I won't tell Wixx that I found you in here if you suck me off? Right here. Right now."

I spit in his face. "You have two seconds to release me or I scream bloody murder." I can feel the sweat roll down my back as his grip tightens.

"Ronald! Are you insane? Get your hands off her!" Wixx storms in, observing the scene. The pervert lets me go. I run behind the desk, rubbing my wrists and grab the charity ball folder.

"She was snooping in your stuff, sir. I caught her red-handed." Ronald whines.

"Ms. Dedano?" Wixx looks at me.

"I brought you the contracts to sign off on for the charity ball. Here they are." I'm fighting to keep my composure and winning at the moment.

Ronald looks down at his shoes while Wixx tears him a new asshole for touching me and frightening me. Now guilt creeps in that he's defending my honor with such sweetness.

Ronald gets banished to his quarters, and Wixx closes the door behind him. He slithers up to me and I jump as his fingers button the top buttons of my blouse. "So beautiful and sexy. I cannot blame Ronald for wanting a desirable woman like you. Every guy in the room wants you wherever you go. I can sense it when we're out together. Being with you amplifies my already firm sense of power." He twirls a curl in my hair and his peppermint breath bathes my cheek. "No one may touch you while I'm around to protect you. We're a team now, Gem."

I dare not cringe or move away. I stay stone still, not even swallowing. Wixx kisses my forehead and moves to sit.

"Let's check the contracts—"

"No, I'm positive it can wait until tomorrow. Wanted you to have them on your arrival in the morning. You'll be late. I, um … heard Ronald say he was supposed to drive you."

"Would you like to join us for dinner?"

"Oh, no thank you. Both my girlfriend and I have plans to do something together."

"It wouldn't be a date you're not telling me about, would it?" He rises and invades my personal space again. It almost feels as threatening as the chauffeur, but I act as if I like it. He cannot know I'm betraying him and this is how I keep him thinking I'm in his corner.

"Of course not! I read my copy—I won't accompany another man in public until our contract ends."

"Correct. That's why I pay you your six-figure salary. We must appear the happiest couple. The investors thrive on that." He runs a finger down my bare arm. "In fact, I've booked a dance lesson for us. It's so we look polished and in sync on the dance floor."

I give him my biggest smile. "Sounds like fun."

"We start tomorrow. Get some sexy dancing shoes."

"Sure, I will."

He places his hand at the small of my back and walks me out. We stop in the hallway as he locks the deadbolt. Then he accompanies me to my car.

"Take the morning off tomorrow to get your dress and shoes. Have them on during our lesson. Here, use this…" He hands me his Black Centurion American Express card. "I've already cleared you to use it."

"Thanks, but it's unnecessary to—"

"Gemma, do as I say and find the perfect dress and shoes. Or I'll have to take you shopping myself. Is that what you want?" He's leaning into the window of my car and drops his head. "I'll pick you up at ten a.m."

"Wait, that's unnecessary. Really." I shake my head with force.

He shakes his head with a sly grin. "I've decided, little one. Everything must be perfect for our debut as a couple." He leans in and kisses my forehead, dismissing me.

Driving home, I don't even know how I got here. I'm exhausted. The Feds are waiting for me with smiles.

"You did great! The conversation between you, the chauffeur, and Wixx came through loud and clear," Frost says.

"I was contemplating busting in and saving you from that asshole. But Wixx beat me to the punch," Cross says.

"Now, Cross, you know that would have blown our case sky high," Frost says. "Gemma would have handled him just fine."

Weary from the events of the day, I sigh. "Gentlemen, I'm going to bed. Please leave."

The next morning, Wixx is right on time. Billy keeps calling and texting. I had to turn off my phone. I stuff it in my purse before getting into the limo. Ronald is not the chauffeur, surprise. Wixx slides up next to me, putting his hand on my knee. He smells amazing.

"Good morning, sleep well?" His posture is confident, legs spread wide, his opposite arm languishing over the seat back.

"Yes, thanks. Did you fire Ronald?" I turn in my seat to face him.

"I eliminated that pervert right after you left last night. But don't worry, I gave him a big sendoff." He flicks his wrist.

"What kind of sendoff?"

"The kind with lots of zeros attached. We don't want him blaming you and coming around again. So, I paid him off." He tries to reel me back in his grasp with his arm around my shoulders.

"Wow, that was very kind of you. I was a little apprehensive about seeing him today." I let myself relax a little.

"No doubt. I expected that would be the case. You should always feel safe in my care. I will see to it." He pulls me closer into him in a side hug.

We pull up to the Neiman Marcus on Michigan Avenue as the driver opens my door. There's an elderly lady, impeccably dressed from head to toe, waiting outside for us. A short, petite assistant with a tablet next to her.

"Mr. Wixx, we are so honored you are here today. Please follow me."

A doorman opens the door. We find ourselves in a boardroom-like area. In one corner, there's a dressing area with a central platform and a three-way mirror. A rolling rack holds numerous evening gowns, along with accompanying shoes.

They make Wixx comfortable on a plush down filled chair with a glass of champagne. I'm led into the dressing room with a sales associate.

"Is there a preference we need to address for you, Ms.?" she asks.

"I haven't thought about it. Just throw stuff at me and I'll try it on." I shrug.

"Great idea. I think Mr. Wixx will have the last word. Yes?" Her painted-on eyebrows rise.

"Yes."

While many women would jump at the chance to recreate Julia Roberts' Pretty Woman experience, I'm uninterested and find it exhausting. With clothes, dressing for comfort is my jam. I acknowledge exceptions and acquiesce when necessary, but this obsession with clothing is absurd. I'm thinking he just wants to ogle me.

He ends up picking a vibrant blue slip of a dress that has to be worn with only the smallest thong or risk lines showing through. There's no possibility for even a stick-on bra with this plunging neckline. I'll have to tape the dress to myself so I don't fall out. The silk feels as if baby angels spent years weaving it into the thin fabric.

The sales associate kneels to put the shoes on me. "These cost more than my car," she whispers. I shake my head and motion for her to get up. I can buckle my own shoes, for fuck's sake.

"Perfection, my dear. You will turn heads for sure in that dress," Wixx says. Just as in the car, he's taking up space on the sofa, legs and arms spread wide.

"Thank you, it's beautiful." I force a smile.

"Now we need cruise wear. Please select a weekend's worth of outfits for a vacation."

I don't have the opportunity to question him or balk at the request. I try nothing of it on. The pile is complete in no time and Wixx pays.

The saleswomen wave us off as we get picked up. There's hope the commission is enough to make the fact that they kissed our asses a distant memory. I keep the shoes on for the day to be ready for our dance lesson later this afternoon.

"You never mentioned a vacation. I don't know if—I've never left the city of Chicago." I attempt to unclench my fists.

His eyebrows raise. "Haven't you ever taken a vacation?"

I tilt my head and tap my finger on my bottom lip. "Not unless you count the time I hid under the front porch from my mother's boyfriend."

"Dedano never took you anywhere?" His eyes widen.

"He was busy building an empire. You know how that is." I shrug. "Oh, I forgot. I went to Vegas for a bachelorette party once."

He screws up his lips. "Your mother, didn't she try to protect you as a little girl?"

"My mother wasn't cognizant most of my life. Thank goodness my grandma took me away from her. It was the only chance I had of living past my preteen years." My neck muscles are tight, so I rotate my head in a circle.

"How sad. I have to admit that my mother was the exact opposite. She was the only person I've truly ever loved." Wixx has a glazed look.

Car stops, the door opens, we're at The Trump International Hotel and Tower. The establishment, named Sixteen after the floor, is where we have lunch rubbing elbows with the super-rich. We enjoy a sophisticated dining experience while taking in views of the Chicago River and skyline.

"Are you having fun spending the day with me? This is us getting comfortable with one another to convince the masses we're an intimate couple." He gives me a playful grin, pretending to brush away a strand of hair from my temple.

"I'm not sleeping with you, Wixx." I smirk.

"Are you sure? I think maybe you'll beg to one day." He smirks back, now putting his hand on my thigh.

I giggle at his joke. "Go ahead, keep trying, Mr. Flirty, but I've never begged in my life and I don't intend to start now." He runs a finger down my bare arm. As I slap his hand away, a mischievous glint flashes in Mr. Flirty's eyes. He chuckles, a low, seductive sound that sends shivers down my spine.

Wixx is charming and handsome, an excellent conversationalist, sometimes even sexy. In another life where Billy didn't exist, I might have given him a fair chance. He orders a second bottle of wine and I realize I need to cut back. Once, I could out drink any man, but my tolerance has decreased since I turned my life around. I don't want to slip.

As I gaze around the restaurant, I notice a sprinkling of celebrity patrons. I straighten my posture and take a sip of wine. I'm not intimidated by rich people because I was one once. But celebrities make me nervous.

"Don't look now, but Paulo Patrino is coming our way." Wixx places his hand on top of mine. I play along.

"The famous director?" I whisper.

He nods and rises from his seat to greet the gentleman. Then he introduces me with only my name and no descriptive words who I am to him.

"Pleasure to meet you, Gemma." The guy kisses the back of my hand.

"How's the new movie going?" Wixx asks.

"Perfection. We landed Bianca Belle in the lead." He smiles with all his blinding white teeth. "I'll see you at the ball next week, Wixx. I hope to see you as well, Gemma."

He walks away as I smile back. It was a quick and exciting flyby.

"How do you know him?" I ask.

"I invest his money, my dear." He leers.

I nod and sip my wine. Wixx fills my glass as soon as I set it down. Lunch arrives and we're both starving, so it's quiet while we take our first bites. Then Wixx interrupts my fascination with my salad.

"I hope you enjoy the dance lesson. In no time, Marguerite will have us in sync."

"Maria bought us dance lessons at Innamorare so we could look sophisticated to our high-class clients." I wink at him. "So, I know a few moves."

"Great, we'll be the best dancers there, no doubt." A little squeeze of my thigh for intimacy's sake.

"Gemma, this is Marguerite, our dance instructor." Wixx says as the woman approaches, arms out to hug him. She's more his age than mine, but in amazing shape. Her body is all muscle. She's wearing a leotard with a flowing skirt over it. Her shoes are much more dance appropriate than mine. I'm used to maneuvering in stilettos so I'm not worried.

Inwardly, I grin at how long the hug lasts between them. It's evident that she's attracted to the billionaire. What woman wouldn't? He's handsome, charming and rich.

"Pleasure to meet you, Marguerite," I greet her with a polite handshake.

She shakes my hand, returning the greeting. But since her attention revolves around Wixx, I might as well be invisible. Marguerite wastes no time putting her hands on Ben to teach us the first dance. They accomplish a dramatic tango while I watch. She wears an eager look, like a dog with a dangling bone. Or it might just be that she painted her eyebrows much too high on her forehead. Not sure.

I clap at the show and walk over to Wixx. He has an amused look on his face at my boldness. "I can tango too." His eyebrows peak and he licks his lips, holding out his arms for me to get into hold. Marguerite starts the music and true to form, Wixx takes on the seductive demeanor of the Tango. Our dance moves are seamless, as if we've been partners forever. I'm immersed in the world of provocative dance, head woozy from the wine. He twirls me and performs the steps like a sexual rendezvous, our legs, and arms entangled beautifully. The music comes to the end, and he dips me into a seductive drop, holding me in his powerful arms for a beat too long. *Fuck, Wixx is sexy.*

Twenty-Three

BILLY

"We have to expose Wixx for the fuckin snake that he is," Joe says, taking a sip of Scotch. We're in my living room drinking to dull the pain of the loss we had at the council meeting today.

"How will you manage to get something on him?" I shake my head.

"I don't know—maybe set him up? But I can't risk losing my license dealing with illegal shit." He sits in the white leather chair and crosses his ankle over his knee.

"I can't waste any further time on this asshole today. Gem still won't talk to me." I send her another text. "She's fuckin ghosting me. And I'm clueless why, since I rocked her world the last night we were together." I move the pillows Gemma picked for our sofa and sit, placing my drink on the coffee table.

Joe laughs. "Maybe she needs to right her axis before she'll speak to you again." He bites his bottom lip with a big, asshole smile behind it.

The harder he laughs, the more I kick his chair. His phone interrupts our banter. "Hello. Hey, Ian. Yeah, I'm at Billy's. What time? OK, we'll be there tonight. See you then."

"What's up with Ian?" I grab my glass and take a sip.

"Ian's coming to the club. Eve's giving him the night off of daddy duty." Joe stands, clapping his hands. "Hey, I've got it! We can arrange for Ian to bring down Wixx for us."

"Wixx would never see it coming." I point my index finger at him. "Brilliant idea."

"We can discuss it with him tonight." He walks to the door and says, "I'll be there at 10 o'clock. Don't be late because you're fucking your wife."

"If I'm fucking my wife … you assholes can wait." I flip him off.

After Joe leaves, I go out on my deck and look at the lake. I can remember many nights sitting out here with Gemma. Sometimes, we'd make love in the gazebo. Her silken hair in the moonlight was like spun gold. The curls would fan out over her like a crown as we fucked. There was nobody nearby to hear her scream my name when she climaxed again and again.

It was there, at the gazebo, where she first mentioned wanting a divorce. She voiced it three times before she left me. How I wanted to purge that from my brain. She was out here when I arrived home from work late one night. Oblivious to her problems with our marriage, I carried on with my business as usual.

"Hey, what's for dinner? I'm starving." I popped a grape in my mouth from the bowl on the way through the kitchen.

"I stopped making dinner for a husband who leaves me to eat alone every night." She downed the remnants of a glass of whiskey.

"Please, Gem, don't start with all that stuff now. I had an awful day and just need to unwind. I'll make myself something, no problem. You want anything?"

"Yes, a divorce." Her voice was full of venom. But then changed to a cry at the end of the declaration.

My jaw was so tight I thought I'd crack a molar. I made two fists and stretched out my fingers. Without acknowledging that dirty word, I went inside and poured myself a bowl of cereal. Eating alone in front of the television was my punishment for becoming a successful entrepreneur. I didn't take her seriously back then. Now, it's fuckin everything.

Later that evening, I arrive at the club to spot Joe and Ian already there. I ask them both to come to my office so we can discuss how to handle Wixx. I unlock the steel door and wave them to the leather chairs in front of my desk. One-way glass overlooks the dance floor and the bar behind their heads.

"I can't believe his name is Benny Soto. He's been trying to persuade me to invest with him for years. There was always a questionable element attached to him, so I ignored his calls. I had no idea how much of a snake he is," Ian says. "I can talk to him at the charity ball. We're attending this weekend for the children in the cancer ward. Wixx is throwing the whole thing. In fact, Gemma called Eve and asked for help with the preparations."

"Fuck, that means he's gonna be parading my Gem around on his arm like his girlfriend." I pound my fist on the desk.

"I told you to come clean with her," Joe says. "Ian, can you believe this idiot faked his divorce?" Joe swivels his chair toward Ian and points at me over his shoulder with his thumb.

"That sounds fucked up, Billy. Gemma thinks she's a free agent to engage in whatever she wants. What if she's exercising those freedoms? How you feeling about that?" His eyes are wide with accusation.

After a loud exhale, I rub the back of my neck with my palm. "She's already done that while she worked with Maria. I accepted it when she returned. Now, I'm sleeping with her again. It damn well better not be Wixx too. I'll fucking kill the bastard."

Joe plays with the trophy on my shelf. "Get a handle on it before it's too late."

"I'll investigate and see what I can find out at the charity ball." Let's not lose faith in Gem. "Eve says she wants to succeed at her new job, and sleeping with the boss is not a good start," Ian says. "I can even arrange for Eve to ask her to lunch. She'll uncover the truth about Gem's situation."

"Thanks Ian, I owe you, man. She won't even answer my calls." My head is down, nodding.

"That's what friends are for." He holds his hand out to shake and then pulls me in for a bro hug. "I gotta go. Promised Eve I'd be back before she goes to sleep." He winks at us both.

"Go enjoy your hot wife," Joe says and Ian leaves. Joe paces in the room a bit, which always makes me crazy. But I guess it's his process, like when he's in court. "Fuck, I was just thinking about the day you took me with you to pick out Gemma's ring. I remember saying to myself that you two would be together forever."

"I'm determined to bring her back, no matter what. And turn that thought into reality." I poke the wood desk with the tip of my letter opener.

"Once Ian discovers where you stand, we should brainstorm a more creative approach beyond just calling and texting her." Joe picks up my phone, making his point.

"Every time we meet up, we end up having sex. I need to find a way to meet."

"It'll have to be she shows up thinking the meeting is with someone else, or a surprise visit to her place."

"Wait ... what if I convince her to agree to be fuck buddies?" I stand with my arms out at my sides. "I'll create the illusion that I won't let my feelings enter it. Just mutual sexual satisfaction. I'll keep satisfying her until she wakes up and realizes that the sex is amazing because she's still in love with me."

"Who do you think you are? David Copperfield? How the fuck will you manage to do that? You're delusional." Joe closes his eyes and shakes his head.

I plop back into my seat. "I'm desperate."

Twenty-Four

GEMMA

I might as well be taping hundred-dollar bills to my body. That's the level of attention I'm going to attract with this dress. The vibrant blue silk glides over me and fits me like a glove. I rely on body tape to avoid any embarrassing nip slips. The smallest wisp of a thong is a must because I refuse to go total commando to a kid's charity ball. As I gaze in the mirror, I can perceive why Wixx selected this particular garment. It's because he wants every man in the place lusting after me. I'm no stranger to that feeling. Having stripped naked many times on stage, I even enjoyed it. So tonight, just like any other on stage, I'm gonna own it. Be proud of my appearance and youthful glow.

I never experienced praise from others anywhere else in my life. Unless one of my mom's boyfriends wanted to grope me. I realized they were grooming me to earn my trust. Falling for that trick once teaches you a valuable lesson. After being ignored by my mother, and abused by her boyfriends, by the moment my grandma came to save me, the damage was already done.

Other kids ridiculed and mocked me because I was tall and painfully skinny. Meals were few and far between. My grandma tried her hardest to feed me when my mom would disappear for days. The first time I got my period, I remember being scared and in shock, crying in the restroom at the grocery store. A nice lady helped me by buying me new underpants and the feminine products I needed. She stayed outside the stall and explained the steps to take when I had questions. When I stepped out, she wiped my tears and made me wash my hands and face. She told me she was proud of me for following directions so well. After a long while she left, I wished with all my heart she was my parent instead of the one I received.

When Billy entered my world, I had already accepted being solely a sexual being. One that dedicated themselves to maintaining my figure for the customers to admire and lust after. Anything I acquired or accomplished was because of my looks. So, I learned to use it as currency to make ends meet. This is no different. Wixx is paying me to use my looks to seduce rich people into letting him invest their money.

As I sit on the chair to buckle the ankle strap on my shoe, he knocks.

"Come in."

He enters the guest room I'm using in his mansion as my dressing room. "You're stunning!" Before I can say anything, he kneels before me and buckles my shoe.

"Wixx, you don't ha…"

"Nonsense. Touching your gorgeous legs is the only excuse I have." He pops up to his feet, grabs both my hands, and pulls me up. He faces us toward the mirror and stands behind me.

"Look at that power couple. No one can refuse us." Then he places a diamond necklace on my throat and clasps it from behind me. I touch it with my fingers, in awe of its beauty. It's rare these things impress me when I see other women wearing them, but I comprehend what his agenda is for the ball and go with it.

"I can tell what you're thinking, Gem." Don't worry, it's on loan because it belonged to my mother. She was very ill, and I had just made my first million. I wanted to bring a smile to her face, giving her what I knew she deserved.

"That's sweet, Wixx. It's fine. I'm all for helping you accomplish your goals tonight. Lead the way." I gesture with my hand.

He places both palms on my bare arms with a gentle squeeze and kisses my neck. A little heat rises in my core and it's weird. But when he turns me to face him, I realize why … Wixx in a tuxedo is fuckin hot. Any red-blooded female would appreciate the view and feel a slight tingle.

Upon arrival, the attendant directs our limo to the head of the line. People gather round as we exit the car. Wixx comes around to grab my wrist and I emerge ladylike without a peep show of my crotch. Believe me, I was worried because the dress isn't leaving much to work with in the coverage department. He snatches me under his arm, silencing everyone's questions about our relationship.

"This is my girlfriend, Gemma." He introduces me to everyone in the ballroom. Some delight in meeting me, some are condescending, which I'm used to. One lady never approaches us, but her eyes never divert from me. She has a scowl on her face. I try not to let it cause me discomfort.

Soon after dinner, Wixx leads me to the floor where we tango. I'm surprised when the crowd opens up to watch only us. Wixx devours the recognition. He intensifies the dance's intimacy and sensuality. I'm caught up in his handsome charisma and have forgotten the true reason I'm here when he dips me at the end. He kisses me and I kiss him back.

The music ends, and at the edge of the dance floor are Ian and Eve. "Wow, that was some tango." Eve locks arms with me while Ian speaks to Wixx. We head out onto the balcony for some privacy. "What's going on with you and Benjamin Wixx? Is it serious?"

"No … I'm playing a part… It's a requirement of my position he hired me for. He parades me as his girlfriend, expecting me to attract clients with charm and beauty." I flutter my eyelashes and she cracks up.

"Well, you look amazing, girl. There isn't an investor in there can say no to you." She animatedly looks me up and down as I laugh and strike a pose.

"Aww, thanks. I'm having fun while I'm at it." I shrug.

"Just don't fall for the handsome crooked billionaire. You're aware that he's a criminal, correct?" Using her index finger, she punctuates her point.

"I'm aware, Billy pounded it into me like a hammer. I informed him, like I'm informing you—I can look after myself."

"I'm certain that you can! Good luck." She hugs me.

Ben finishes his conversation with Ian and he's at my side once more. "How about some more champagne?" He holds a full glass in front of me.

"Are you trying to get me drunk? Mr. Wixx, you know I won't sleep with you," I whisper in his ear.

"Can't blame me for trying, can you?" He holds his arms out to his sides with a vibrant smile.

I laugh, and he sips the champagne. We dance the rest of the evening away. He is the ideal sexy partner I could become accustomed to dating if this were reality. He enjoys PDA, so I allow him to come close, touch, and give occasional kisses. Sitting through a meal while he caresses my inner thigh and twirls my hair is like he's marking me as his. It's all a show for the investors, right?

The last song ends for the night, and I visit the ladies' room. When I emerge from the stall to go to the sink, she's standing right there, glaring at me in the mirror. The woman I lost track of who was stalking us earlier.

"He's a con artist and a criminal. Kick him to the curb or end up the victim like me. You're just his whore. He's using you just as he did to me." Her index finger is in my face and I slap it aside.

"Don't make assumptions about things you know nothing about. Leave me alone."

"I have the means to exact my revenge on old Benny Soto. Bet you weren't informed that's his real name. He crossed the wrong bitch when he picked me. Stay away from him or else."

"Are you seriously threatening me? You've got balls, bitch—I'll give you that." I dodge around her to the sink.

"It's not a threat, it's a promise! I'm taking down Benjamin Wixx and if you're with him, you'll suffer the same fate, too." That warning comes from her reflection in the mirror.

She's close on my heels as I try to exit. Using her foot, she prevents the door from opening. "Remember, you don't want to become a casualty in the crossfire. I would hate to see this pretty face and body blown to bits. Make the right decision." She pushes the door and me out of the way. I'm taken aback by her threat to blow us up. What do I do? Call homeland security? Tell Wixx?

I shut the entrance of the ladies' room and lock it. Then I fish my phone out of my purse and call the Feds.

"This is Cross … I'm so glad you called Gemma."

"What does that mean?" I set my bag down on the counter.

"We believe there's been a hit arranged for an attack on Wixx's life. Are you still in the event hall?"

"I'm in the restroom right now. A bitchy lady threatened to blow up Wixx. She was warning me to steer clear of him. What am I supposed to do?" My hand squeezes my phone like a vise.

"First, examine the photo I'm sending you and tell me if this is the individual." I remove it from my ear and view the picture on the screen.

"Yes! That's her."

"Good girl, we have a positive ID and can pick her up. But we still need to keep you protected and far from him. There is a stairwell right outside the door. Take it to the bottom level in the garage. Frost and I will wait for you there and escort you to a secure location."

"OK, what if Wixx is waiting just outside?" I rub my forehead.

"Text him you were sick and Eve Ansaldo took you home."

"OK, hold on."

I make it quick and text Wixx before returning to Cross.

> Gemma: I'm not feeling well. Eve and Ian are taking me home. She was in the bathroom with me when I became ill and insisted.

> Wixx: I hate the night ended with you getting sick. Will you be alright alone?

> Gemma: I'll be fine. Nothing I haven't experienced before after excessive drinking. I'll see you at work on Monday morning, bright and early.

> Wixx: Get some rest, I'll send over some soup for you tomorrow.

I end the message with an emoji and he's OK with it all. I hope.

"Cross? I'm coming down... have you guys arrived yet?" I grab my purse, heading towards the exit.

"Something's happened and we can't come. I'll send an officer for you."

I stop myself from opening the lock. Can't leave the washroom until I have an escape plan. A cop car will draw too much attention.

"No, that won't be necessary. I have a ride with a friend." *I just lied to a Fed. Crap!*

"We just received information that your ex-husband is there. He's looking for you and we can't risk that he and Wixx will engage in an altercation. Frost and I are leaving at this moment, and we have security on site to intervene. Gemma, I cannot say this with any more authority in my voice—Maintain your distance from Wixx!"

"I promise, I will until you notify me the coast is clear." I sit on the upholstered chair in the bathroom's vestibule.

"Make your way to the hotel address in my text. The key will be waiting for you at the check-in desk. Stay at that location until we have more information. Confirm if your friend can stay with you. Text me when you're safe inside. I'll be in touch, gotta go. Goodbye."

Fuck, why is Billy here? I refuse to let anything happen to him. That would be just as bad as getting caught in the crossfire myself.

Texting him, I try to work through the angst and pray he answers…

Gemma: Don't tell anyone I'm texting you. Stop arguing with Wixx!!! Please help me. I'm hiding in the ladies' room. I told Wixx I went home sick, so keep that a secret. Meet me at the bottom floor of the hotel garage in five minutes with your car. Please Billy! This is important. Avoid getting anywhere near Wixx!

Billy: Why the fuck are you hiding? What did he do to you? I'll fucking kill him when I find him!

Gemma: NOOOOO! STAY AWAY FROM WIXX!!! I need you now. Come pick me up and I'll explain later.

Billy: Coming right now! You're my top priority.

Twenty-Five

BILLY

Gemma is right where she told me she'd be, in the lower-level garage. She must be freezing because she's grasping her coat around her body. The wind off of Lake Michigan whips through these cement structures. I pull up and jump out of the vehicle to her side, and she steps of her own free will into my arms. It's clear that she is shaken. I hug her tight, never wanting to let go.

"What's happening? Why were you hiding?"

She steps back as if some lightning bolt of courage hit her. "Hurry, I'll explain later." I open the door and she slides into the seat. She links her mobile to the car's GPS.

"Follow the directions." She breathes in, closing her eyes and wrapping her arms around herself.

Only the GPS's artificial voice speaks the entire route to our destination. She stays for the duration of the ride, eyelids closed, hugging herself. I'm not yet on solid ground with her, so I'm giving her some space.

When we arrive, she sits up straight as if nothing has happened. She pops out of the car before I can say a word. Gem is so stunning, so statuesque. She steals my breath when she comes back out from the lobby with the keys to a suite. I drive to the building's other side, valet, and we ride the elevator to the floor.

"Hey, babe, you didn't have to resort to a cry for help to convince me to join you on a rendezvous in a hotel," I joke.

There's a slight grin on her face as she shakes her head at me. "It wasn't fake. I needed you and you came without pause. That's all that matters to me." Her palm rests on her heart.

Her emotions are all over the place. From scared and seeking a hug, to take charge and acquire the key, to appreciative and humble. What the fuck is going on? I'm completely clueless about how to react. So, I will communicate the same thing I've been telling her—the truth. She pivots and leads the way inside. The suite is identical to any hotel of this caliber, affordable and efficient. Gem walks to the window and closes the thick blackout drapes while I flip on the light switch.

Resting my fingertips on her shoulders, I need her full attention. "Gem, I've put you as my only priority. I'll be here whenever you need me."

"I'm seeing that. But we have a long road ahead. You led me to experience a sense of worthlessness and unimportance. I swore no one would compel me to become that person again. But I'm grateful you're trying to make things up to me."

"I'm sorry. Showing you is all I can do now." I help her off with her coat … Wow. Gemma is wearing a skin tight blue dress. It flows like butter over every curve and her tits are looking delicious. "You look incredible. That dress for me?" Backing her up to the far wall, I corral her with my body. Her scent, the sensation of her silky curls against my skin, her increasing breath. It all brings back so many memories.

"Don't flatter yourself Dedano." She maintains a forced expression of indifference but doesn't engage in any action to push me away. Another one of her mood switches. I'm suffering from whiplash but it's making me hard.

"It's amusing how you're once again eager to call me by my last name. Is first name basis off the table at this time? What should I call you?" I trace her collarbone with my index finger.

"Call me whatever the fuck you want. I don't care." She turns her head and twists her lips.

I direct her gaze back to mine by using the same finger under her chin. "How about I make you call me God like you used to?" I kiss her neck and lick her earlobe just the way she likes it.

Her palms shift from shoving me off at my chest to my ass. She's smashing my erection against her as we kiss. It's rough, primal, where I can't wait to see this sexy scrap of silk on the floor. She lets me unzip it. I admire her after it falls to the floor. Gem is the most beautiful woman I've ever seen. Her curves are perfection all the way up to her naked gorgeous tits. Legs that go on forever and that ass is fucking sublime. The almost invisible scrap of silk she wears as underwear shimmies down to the floor, leaving her naked.

"Less looking, more fucking!" She pushes me backward onto the bed. Oh, how I love the Gem that is feisty and controlling. I'm shocked, as she is so efficient at removing my clothes and then straddles me on the bed. But I snap to my senses when she fondles my dick before placing it where she wants it. Her hips keep rhythm as her hair falls down around our faces. My palms graze up her sides to worship her breasts and pinch her nipples to hard tips.

I turn us both over and increase the intensity of my thrusts with more passion. I know just how Gem likes it and what buttons to push to bring her to climax.

"Oh, God! Yes, make love to me, Billy. It's been too long. Fuck me harder. Oh, God, that's it! Don't stop."

There it is! I never thought I'd hear her call me God one more time. Soon after, I reach nirvana inside my Gemma, as we did many times before. In this instance, a subtle difference was evident.

"It's still as amazing as when we first met." I place small kisses down her cleavage.

"It's late, you should leave." We've gone from devil sex nymph to ice princess. She gets out of bed and throws on her dress. "Just promise me you'll steer clear of Benjamin Wixx."

"How about you avoid my worst enemy as well? His sole purpose is revenge on me and my family. He just maneuvered the board to give him the casino instead of me." I stand up and jump into my pants.

"Things like that may not be important at this moment... I'm trying to say... I understand it's important to you and the company. But…" She's gazing at her reflection in the mirror while removing the diamond choker she's wearing.

"Did Wixx give you that necklace? Aren't you tired of this? Why are you here all alone? When did you move out of the apartment you were living in? Why haven't you used the funds I provided in your account to secure a permanent place?"

"You still don't get it! I don't need your money! I'll never use that account." Gem doesn't turn around.

"Then move back home with me. What just happened proves we should continue to be together."

"See ya later. I have to get some sleep." She plays with her jewelry on the dresser. I realize I have once again lost her.

"There are two options here. We patch things up for good, or I'm giving up on you. I really mean it." A sick wave of nausea crawls up my body after saying that to her.

"You really mean it this time? Funny, I heard this all before." She faces me, waving her arms. I grab hold of her hands and position them on my chest, bringing us face to face.

"Look, I don't care about the past. I messed up, yeah. Just forgive me and let's move on."

Tears fill her gaze before she breaks free of my hold and turns her back on me for another time. "You have to accept the fact that it might not be possible. You hurt me deep."

After removing them, she places her earrings on the dresser with the necklace. "In the beginning, you coerced me into accepting your caring and attention when I was satisfied with just sex. Then I fell in love with you and we have our whirlwind wedding—But after a while all the love, caring, and devotion from you disappeared. I couldn't bear it—reverting to the version of myself I was before. Ignored, unworthy, and alone. I kept my promise to reveal to you what's on my mind. But you stopped honoring your commitment to listen."

I approach her from behind, my front against her back. "Let's hash it out. Get everything out here and now. I'll stay in this hotel room with you for however many days it takes. But I need you to want that, want … me."

She inhales, tilting her chin to feel my lips against her collarbone. Silent for a few seconds, then she spins with force, pushing me aside. Back to ice princess. I rub my poor neck. This whiplash will be the death of me.

"So, two options? This is an ultimatum? Are you a child?" Her expression is tight.

"If you won't admit you want this to work, why am I here? You called me." My arms are out at my sides, palms facing her.

"You don't understand." She bites her lip with intensity.

"What are you trying to tell me, Gem?" Sitting on the bed, I run my fingers through my hair.

"There are things you're unaware of. And I can't tell you." Gemma studies the carpet.

"There's my answer then. I'm done."

I grab my shirt, moving to leave. "No more showing up at my clubs. Stay away from me." I open the door. "I can't be around you and not have you in my life."

"Wait! I'm hiding out here." Gem's attitude changes to tired and defeated. Her rough, callous demeanor gone. "I had to separate you from him."

I close the door. "Are you in danger? Why didn't you say so?"

"No. No, I don't think so?" Her voice rises at the end of the sentence, suggesting a question about her safety. When her phone rings and she's quick at picking it up. "Hello. Hold on a second." She takes the call in the bathroom with the faucet running.

"Who was that?" My question comes out a little too harsh.

"It was Eve." I've always been able to sense when Gem lies. She looks at her nails.

"Hmm, you won't tell me what's happening?"

"I believe it's best not to." She shakes her head.

"How can we work on getting back together when you won't confide in me?" I close the distance between us. "Give me the phone." I grab it out of her hand. "You're still intending to see him? Work for him ... Even though you know he's striving to ruin me?"

She can't even glance at me. "Just … Can't you trust me?"

"Trust you? How can I trust you when you lie to me about who's on the phone?" I throw the device on the bed.

"It's just work. He wanted to inquire about a project I was working on for him today." She shrugs like it's no big deal.

"What boss calls his employee at two in the morning? That was a hook up request. A come fuck me. Wasn't it? You were gonna jump from our bed to his…" I snap my fingers. "Just like that."

"No, we've never fucked! I told you I'm never sleeping with him." Her hand slices through the air. "Listen, there's nothing to worry about. I have it all under control."

"What's under control? I swear to fuck if you don't come clean this instant. I'm determined to confront him myself. What's the big secret?" I clench my fists a few times.

"YOU! OK? You! Because if anything were to happen to you. I'd … I could never forgive myself. OK? So, just forget it and trust me." She slumps, studying the floor below.

"Gem, I don't depend on you to protect me. I hate you think I can't handle myself. Either you inform me of everything that's going on or I walk and find out the news elsewhere."

"Fine! God! Fine! I'll tell you. Two feds approached me after I started working for Benjamin Wixx. They are making me help them bring him down. If I don't, they were considering investigating you as an accomplice."

"So let them! I'm an open book. Why would you risk your own safety to keep the feds off my back?" We're toe to toe at this moment. Her eyebrows crease and she averts her gaze.

"You like him! Don't you? You've wanted him since the day you met him, haven't you?" I grasp her bicep and pull her towards me.

"Jealousy doesn't look good on you, Billy." She rolls her eyes.

"Remember what I said about rolling your eyes at me? I have no patience for that. Don't deflect on me. Admit it! You're attracted to him. You thought he'd be the one to save you from yourself." I sit on the bed. "That was supposed to be me. Not him."

"Except you couldn't set aside some hours from your empire to prioritize me. He has done that." That sentence just ripped out my guts and stomped them on the floor.

"But yet you're trying to take him down with the Feds?" I place my face in my hands and run my fingers through my hair. Look up at her and wait for a response.

Her gaze travels up to me with tear-filled eyes. “I don’t love him, Billy. There’s only one person I’ve ever been in love with in my entire life.”

Twenty-Six

GEMMA

Eight years ago…

My friend Regina is getting married, and the bridal party comprises all exotic dancers. Billy arranges a private jet to take us all to Vegas for Ray's special bachelorette celebration. He's doing very well with his club empire and wants to give something nice to the girls. Regina is thrilled and tells me she's arranged for all of us to stay at The Cosmopolitan.

We fill the weekend with fun things to do together. Every morning we cause a stir at the pool with our parade of thong bikinis. It's becoming comical how early the male population in the hotel is rising for a front seat to the spectacle. Some of us ladies want to work on our tan for the wedding photos. Except Dayo, she has naturally glowing brown skin and uses gallons of sunscreen.

Tonight, we have tickets to see the male strippers. In a fundamental way, the masculine version of what we do for a living. Naked entertainment for the masses. We're all getting dressed and primping for an evening out on the town. Dayo is showering and

Ray and I are perfecting our makeup. As the water turns off, my phone vibrates on the counter. Billy is calling from home to see how we're doing.

"Hey, Gem, how's the bachelorette?" The sounds of the club waking up echo in the background; Vegas is two hours behind Chicago.

"It's been amazing. We're all having a great time and getting well deserved rest. Tonight is the male strip show." I slather on my lip gloss in the mirror as I speak.

"Oh, yeah? Make sure you only think of me while they grind on you." He laughs.

"Without a doubt, you're my one and only male dancer. All I could ever want in a sexy package." Ray nods with enthusiasm at me. Dayo gives a thumbs up through the fog on the glass shower door.

"That's my girl." I can hear Billy's smile in his voice.

"Regina is the one they'll grind on, not me." She slaps my shoulder with her brush. I stick my tongue out at her and walk out of the bathroom for more privacy.

"I'm serious, though. Have a fantastic weekend with your friends. I fucking miss you, babe."

"I miss you too. How about I call you when we return tonight? We can have phone sex." Standing in front of the panoramic windows in our suite, I can observe the lights of Vegas.

"You planning on being fucking horny after watching all those greased up men dance naked?"

"I'm fucking horny right now. None of them will have a better body than you," I giggle.

"That's my Gem! Always ready for action. Call me anytime, baby. I love you."

"Love you too, bye."

We take the limo from dinner to the performance and pile into the theater. We all started drinking early today at the pool, so this should be interesting. The food soaked up some of the alcohol, but they are already serving Ray shots. She has on a sexy skin tight white dress that leaves nothing to the imagination. A sash and a headband with a veil identify her as the bride. I bought them so the dancers can spot her to have her up on stage. I can't wait to witness their expressions when she challenges them by dancing with them. Knowing Regina like I do, for sure she won't be able to enter the spotlight without performing herself.

The music starts, and the men emerge in pants and a jacket. They synchronize their dance moves and transform them into a seductive performance. That's how we differ because we showcase one girl on the pole at a time in our shows. Maybe two once in a while. Here, twelve men are performing, each one hotter than the next. I don't know where to look first.

"Woooooo hoo," Ray screams, waving her arms. Yup, she's toasted.

At about midpoint into the production, they are using harnesses and silks to fly and dance. Regina performs with the silks since Billy took over the club and made it more Vegas like. She's familiar with suspending herself in fabric. They pull her onto the platform and she demonstrates her skills. The audience is cheering for her as if she's part of the show. One of the hottest guys takes center stage with her playing out some erotic moves. She loses the top of her dress in the act, but no one cares. The crowd cheers more. The guys love it because a beautiful woman with a dancer's body and skill is showcasing her talent with them. After that number, she fixes her dress and comes down to us squealing. A twenty-minute intermission ensues.

"You were outstanding!" Dayo says.

"That guy's face when you grabbed the silks and used them as a pro was classic. I have it all on video," I hold up my phone.

"He got turned on, especially when I lost my top. I can't wait to see the replay." She downs the shot the waiter had just brought.

I toast her with my dirty martini, and we sit back down. Another round of shots for the group. A hush comes over the crowd, signaling the intermission is over.

The lights dim, and a piano plays a soft ballad. I recognize it as the band Train's song "Marry Me". I think it's adorable that someone organized this for Regina's wedding. Then the singer's voice fades and a familiar voice starts singing instead. He's behind the piano playing, so I didn't notice him there. I'm in shock to find Billy performing in a Vegas strip club. He's in his usual tight black jeans that make his ass look incredible. A crisp white button-down shirt well-tailored to his muscular torso tops off the Billy Dedano signature look. At the crescendo of the song, he rises from the bench, never missing a syllable. Descending the stairs, he stops in front of me as the last words of the song leave his lips. I have tears streaming down my face when he kneels and presents a black box with a gorgeous emerald-cut diamond ring inside. My heart may just beat right outta my chest and flop right on the floor next to him.

Into the microphone he says, "Gemma Bloom, will you make me the luckiest man on the planet and be my wife?"

I pull him up to his feet and jump him. "Yes, a thousand times. Yes!" I say, as I wrap my arms and legs around his torso like a vise and shower his face with kisses like an eager puppy.

"I love ya, baby. Never want to be without you." He lets my body slide down his firm form to my feet.

The entire venue explodes in cheers for us. He places the ring on my finger and gives me a panty melting kiss with a dip and all. All the bachelorettes gather round and hug us both with congratulations. I'm still in shock.

"Were you surprised?" Regina screams over the loud music. She has tears in her eyes.

"I can't believe you kept it a secret from me. You were helping him the entire time?" She nods and we hug again.

Afterward, Billy takes us backstage to meet all the performers. Turns out two of them were in the bodybuilding competitions with him. All the girls are flirting their asses off. I'm just enjoying my man.

Twenty-Seven

BILLY

Eight years ago…

Gemma comes back to my suite at the Cosmopolitan after the strip club. We both can't stop smiling. She's the most beautiful woman I've ever seen. Her silky blond hair is falling in curls down her back. She has smooth and radiant skin, and her big blue eyes are highlighted with long lashes.

Being a country girl at heart, Gemma loves daisies. I had bunches of the flowers arranged all over the space. When I open the door, she gasps, "Oh, Billy, you did all this?" I nod with a grin. She caresses the white petals with the tips of her fingers. The diamond I just put there winks at me when the light catches it.

The concierge helped me by setting up champagne, strawberries, and chocolate. Also, some other snacks and drinks, and an enormous breakfast to arrive tomorrow morning. Gem loves a hearty breakfast, it's her favorite meal of the day.

She looks in the mirror, holding up her ring on her finger as I come up behind her and enclose her in my arms.

"It's beautiful, but it's too much. You didn't need to spend so much on a ring for me."

"You deserve even more, babe. I love you and want to give you everything."

"All I want is you." She turns and kisses me. Then she charges toward the bathroom, her absence leaving me chilled. "But before I get exactly what I need … you will get your reward for such an amazing proposal."

"Oh! Yeah!" I rub my palms together and follow her.

"Nope." She waves her index finger at me. "Sit in the chair. I'll be right back."

I hold up my hands, moving toward the seat. "Promise I won't move, babe."

Inside the bathroom, music plays from her phone, the Magic Mike theme song that I first danced to for her. The seductive opening beats to the song tells me my Gem is going to give me a private performance, just like I did for her. Her slim, silky leg appears, wrapped around the doorjamb. She runs her hand from her ankle to her thigh. Then Gem splays herself in the doorway, placing each hand on the wood above her. I shake my head and smile when I see she rummaged through my suitcase and stole my white button down. It reaches almost to her knees. She gyrates her hips and pumps them to the beat along with twirling her head.

Stepping into the room, she lifts her long blond hair and quickens her hip movements. She moves her palms to her throat, letting her silky tresses cascade across her shoulders.

Ripping open the dress shirt, she palms her breasts, spilling out of a black lace bra, then down her torso, grabbing her crotch. Her moves mirror the routine in the movie with expert precision. She saunters over to me, teasing me further, her hands doing what I'm longing to do. A sultry dance, never missing a beat. She moves to sit on my lap, provokingly rocking her core against my hard-as-fuck cock.

The little black lace thong panties she knows I love are wet with her arousal. I can't hold back anymore. Ripping those suckers right off of her, I plunge my fingers inside her. Gem's head falls back as she grinds her center on my fingers, seeking the friction of my palm on her clit. She moans, forgetting the dance and the music ending while seeking her orgasm. It appears with a gale wind force, making her scream my name.

"That was hot. I love you, future wifey." She's still breathless perched on my lap.

"Oh, just because you stepped in and interrupted my reward, thank you very much, doesn't mean it's over."

"Baby, I hope not, because my dick is ready to rip these pants in two."

She smiles, then licks her lips while sliding down my body to her knees in front of me. When we make history of my pants, she slides her tongue against my full length and swirls it around the tip. A deep groan of pleasure escapes my lungs as Gem does this better than anyone ever. She's enthusiastic when she licks and tastes every damn inch of me until my hips buck and she knows I'm close. Her mouth comes off with a pop and she hops back up onto my lap, guiding me inside of her. Using the arms of the chair, she pounds herself onto me, going as deep as she can.

I unhook her bra, throwing it across the room and bury my face between her tits. She increases her hip thrusts, knowing I'm at the precipice of ecstasy when I stand holding her body to mine and deposit us both onto the bed.

"This is gonna be the opposite of slow and soft, baby."

A devious smile as she gets up on her knees, sticking that fine ass in my face.

"Yeah, fuck me hard, Billy."

More of the same activities fill the night. Fucking and resting, then eating, drinking, fucking and resting. By the time the morning light becomes evident behind the semi-open blackout drapes, we're delightfully exhausted.

Twenty-Eight

GEMMA

I long to stay in our little bubble together. Our suite at the Cosmopolitan becomes our sanctuary. Designed in muted greys and white, with splashes of sapphire sprinkled into a decor second to none. It even has an attached gym. Billy cannot spend a single day without maintaining his physique. When I try to turn the workout into something sexual, he resists. He arranges for healthy food to be brought up to the room. They also deliver spa treatments to the door. But most of the day and night we're in bed.

My cheek is resting on Billy's chest as I recover from the intensity of yet another orgasm. I'm addicted as if I might be a sexaholic now. It's as addictive as chasing any high like drugs or alcohol.

"It's been three days since we laid eyes on the outside world. Shall we explore and sightsee today?" Billy says.

Finding the strength to lift my head, "What plans would interest me more than what you're packing?" I wiggle my eyebrows and grab his crotch.

He squirms and laughs before answering. "I thought you would want to visit the shops at the Venetian, and then I arranged for us to dine right in front of the Bellagio fountain." He bops my nose with his index finger.

"Dinner sounds great, shopping? Nah."

"Sorry, I forgot you hate shopping. What woman hates shopping?" He shrugs. "My future wife."

"Seeing a magic show has always been a dream of mine. Can we go?" I get up on my knees with the excitement of a child. This is the first time I've ever been anywhere besides Chicago.

"Your wish is my command, my lady."

Billy gets on his laptop and I take a shower. We've been taking showers together for the past three days... A feeling of emptiness pervades. I cannot believe my life is so different in only a couple of years. I expected being alone in old age, similar to my childhood. My man is my everything, and all I desire is his happiness.

"Hey, Gem, I talked to my mom, and she wants us to come to dinner and celebrate the engagement." Billy shouts through the glass enclosure.

OK, I lied. Anything to make him happy but meet the parents … Now what? They're going to ask questions about my family and childhood. Nope, don't want to explore that territory with them. I've built a tough shell around myself to shrug off the opinions of most people. But Billy's family will be mine as well. It bothers me they are required to accept my past as he already has. You can't change the past … I simply don't want to relive it with them so soon.

"Babe? You OK?" It's likely that Billy is wondering why I froze in the shower and resemble a wet statue.

"Um … yeah." I nod. "I'll be right out."

Right after I reply, he is naked and embraces me in his arms beneath the warm water. Now I'm better. He makes me forget all my insecurities when his hands are on me. He leads me to ecstasy and clears my mind. At some point, I'll have to be honest with him.

After drying my hair, I find Billy working on his computer in the main room of the suite. It's now or never. A deep inhale and I burst out with my sentence. "I have some doubts about whether meeting your parents is a great idea for me."

He pops the laptop closed. "What do you mean? They will love you as much as I adore you."

I nibble on my thumbnail, contemplating how I can convey this to him. "Interactions with my friends' families never end well. Since I've never been serious with a guy, this is the first time this has come up for me."

He leads me over to the down filled sofa and sits on an angle facing me so I mirror the same. "Gem, It's crucial to me you are at ease sharing anything with me. Nothing can diminish my love for you, no matter what you do or say."

"OK, well, parents cannot stand me because I lack a stable upbringing. When they ask the typical inquiries, my answers aren't the norm. How often do you see your parents? Did you attend college in Chicago? And the worst, what is your father's occupation? The situation frightens them, leading them to take measures to prevent their child from being in a relationship with someone like me."

"I understand where you're coming from and acknowledge your insecurities. It's okay if you don't feel like meeting them right now. But we're getting married and they will welcome you with open arms, no matter the answers to those questions. They will adore you for the person you are inside." Billy gathers me up into his lap and I place my cheek on his shoulder. "Thank you for telling me the truth, so I won't jump to conclusions."

"Like what?" I grin.

"Well, like you're having second thoughts. Or I did something wrong again." He squeezes me.

"From now on, I promise to tell you what's eating at me."

He grasps my left hand, where my ring sits, and kisses just above. "I promise I'll listen."

Twenty-Nine

GEMMA

Present day…

When I took off my coat and Billy observed me, I had a realization. His eyes roamed from my feet in these expensive torture devices known as shoes, all the way to my face, in an appreciative, hungry perusal. Yes, men often gaze at me with hunger, but this is not the same. How he's always looked at me with pride like I'm his and no one else can change that. It's the same look that makes me believe I'm the most attractive woman in the world. A type of worship no one else ever displayed for me. Furthermore, it brought to mind the guy who had faith in me to oversee his clubs, despite not knowing me very well. Someone who showed confidence in me to take on and triumph over the tough tasks. Gave me credit for my brains, not just my body. He was consistent in making me recognize my worth.

I hate I made him feel inferior to Wixx or anyone else for that matter. There's no chance I'm letting him take a hit to his confidence after he built enough inside me for a lifetime. So, I told him … I told him he's the one and only man I've ever loved. I couldn't decide during the entire conversation, going back and forth between wanting to confess and thinking about pushing him away. I couldn't let him leave, thinking I don't still love him. Because I do.

He stands at the threshold, mouth agape. He closes the door and saunters over to me. With both my hands in his, he lifts me up from the bed. Then he uses his index finger to raise my chin so we're looking into each other's eyes. His always express to me his emotions. We stand looking into each other's souls for a beat.

"YOU, you're the only person." I exhale my anxiety.

"I'm glad you cleared that up. Thank you." His arms surround me like a vise. Like he can't come close enough. He whispers, "You're my only person, too. I love you and that will never change."

We remain silent, basking in the joy of genuine emotions.

"So, we've established how we still feel about each other," he says. Share all the details about Wixx and the Feds so I can ensure your safety.

We sit across from each other, holding hands at the small table. "They instructed me to place listening devices in his office. They say others work for them, but no one is as close to him as me. Now that they are gathering evidence to indict him, won't be long before he goes down."

"Not the first time Benny Soto ends up in jail. He got out before and recreated himself as Benjamin Wixx. He's a slippery crook and they have their work cut out for them."

"The cops might not catch him, but an ex-girlfriend he deceived might. She threatened me in the restroom at the ball."

"What were her exact words?" He squeezes my fingers.

"She warned me to keep my distance from him or risk getting caught in the crossfire. When I informed them, the authorities held suspicions but lacked concrete knowledge about her identity. I ID'd her over the call."

"And when Wixx called you before?" His face screws up.

"He just reached out to ask how I was feeling. He's been very nice to me, in fact." I bite my lip.

"He's a fuckin con artist criminal, of course he's been nice." He pounds on the table and rises to pace.

"OK, let's avoid getting too crazy again. It's all gonna be over soon. They'll arrest him and we'll be done. Let's order some food, and eat together in bed."

Billy calms down and smiles at my suggestion. "I saw an Asian restaurant nearby. I'll pick up Chinese like we used to."

"Chinese in bed ... just like old times." I nod with a grin.

Billy goes for the food and I pull down the bedspread, strip, and snuggle in. The television has nothing to watch, so I flip through the channels until—

BILLIONAIRE BENJAMIN WIXX DIES IN EXPLOSION.

> *"Breaking news... We are at the scene of a vehicle bombing where they suspect the billionaire Benjamin Wixx is the victim in the explosion. Firefighters are working to extinguish the fire. The police are keeping onlookers away from the caution tape," the reporter states.*

Funny feelings emerge in my belly... I'm not sure if it's horror that I should have been in that car? Grief for a friend who treated me well? I even found myself somewhat attracted to him. The job he gave me marked my first legit job, and I excelled. What will I do now?

Nausea overcomes me and I run to the bathroom to empty my stomach contents into the bowl. Tears are falling down my cheeks and sweat covers my brow. Why am I experiencing this reaction to a man's death that everyone said had a connection to wrongdoing? Did I secretly entertain the thought that someone would somehow establish his innocence?

"Gem? I'm here," Billy slams the door, clicking the lock. "What's the matter? You sick?"

I nod, falling further into tears as he picks me up from the floor and places me on the bed. He rushes to the sink and returns with a cold washcloth for my head. Next, he gets a bottled water from the bag he brought to have me drink.

"Thanks. How can you always know what I need?"

"Because a strong thread that will never break attaches us. We can overcome anything together." The comfort induces a fatigue that immerses me in a deep sleep.

I never reveal to him how I questioned my feelings for Wixx. The shock of his murder must be to blame.

Upon awakening, daylight has arrived. Uncertainty is evident in Billy's expression. "Morning, how ya feeling?"

"I'm good. Is everything OK?"

"Um, I have news to tell you. You left the TV on while I held you, and I watched the news. Someone murdered Wixx. Your cellphone buzzed nonstop all morning, but since you were sick, I chose not to disturb you."

Jumping out of bed, I grab my cell from the nightstand. Six messages are from Agent Cross. The most recent was about ten minutes ago. Knocking at the door prompts Billy to toss my dress for me to slip into. I smooth down the wrinkled silk, not having any opportunity to experience embarrassment for wearing last night's clothes.

"Ms. Dedano? Agent Cross here," he says from in the hallway.

I nod and Billy opens up to reveal the two guys I've been working for. Agents Cross and Frost.

"What's he doing here?" Frost says.

I hold up my open palms to calm him and tell them to enter. They sit at the table. Billy stands next to me, arm around my waist. I use him to steady myself.

"My ex-husband is here to guarantee my safety and comfort. He picked me up at the hotel when you failed to." I try to be assertive...

Frost clears his throat. "Well, saves us a trip to question him."

"Go right ahead, I have nothing to hide." Billy straightens his spine.

"A video captures when your vehicle entered the garage where Mr. Benjamin Wixx's limo had been parked before the explosion took place. We think you have a motive for killing him."

"Wait a minute!" I raise my voice like a mother protecting her child because I cannot control my actions. "You both know damn well that the lady who threatened me in the ladies' room caused his death." I move out of Billy's hold and toward the agents.

Billy grabs my wrist and pulls me back into him. "That's fine Gem, I did nothing wrong. They'll learn I'm not to blame." He clears his throat, speaking in his businesslike voice I've heard a million times. "There is a reason my Rolls Royce appeared on that video, being you failed to keep my wife safe when she needed your help. I accomplished that in your absence. What criminal would bring their Rolls to commit a crime? Come on, guys. I'm not a fool. She has fulfilled all your requirements. No need to burden her with this nonsense."

"Do you maintain a grudge against Wixx for stealing the alcohol license from you at the council meeting?" Frost asks sitting back in the chair.

"Ok, how about we relocate this to your offices instead of making my wife upset?" Billy puts out his arm to gesture for them to go.

"We'll be happy to question you in our office."

"I need to bring my wife home, make sure she's doing well. She's been ill."

"You can handle that and meet us later today. You're not under arrest, Mr. Dedano. And as a pillar of the community, I understand you are. I'm certain you'll cooperate."

"Damn right I will. We agreed?" He nods.

"Agreed," Frost repeats.

Billy refuses to drive me to my apartment. Of course, he brings me back to our home. I don't argue, because I can't wait to scrub off that hotel room. And the memory that Benjamin Wixx is dead.

He rushes into the gym, and I can tell he's determined to burn off the frustration. Billy knows how to control his body from the list of foods he eats down to how to control his anger or emotions. He lifts and pushes himself to the limits.

After cleaning up and putting on something comfortable, I make a call. "What's going on there?" I ask the cook at the Wixx mansion. I called as part of my responsibility to maintain employee organization. Cook is the only employee to answer the phone.

"Hello, Ms. D. I am alone here today." She answers in her broken English.

"Are the police there?" I apply some lip gloss while balancing the phone between my shoulder and my ear.

"Everything's gone. They're not here anymore."

"OK, you can go home, too. I will call Ms. Grant and talk to her. Please lock up."

"Yes, Ms. I will."

I call Ben's primary assistant, Roberta Grant. "Hey, Roberta, this is Gemma."

She sobs into the receiver. "He's dead! Did you hear? Of course, you heard what am I saying?"

"Roberta, are you alright? Can I help you with anything?"

"I'm freaked out! Imagine me being in the car with him. I can't return to the house... I'm too scared." She sniffles.

"I'm sure the investigators have examined the property. Cook was present when I phoned."

"She's so loyal she'd stay even if the entire building engulfed in flames." She exhales with force into the phone.

"I gave her permission to return to her home. The place will be empty."

"Further reason I can't go." Her sobs overwhelm her again.

"Take it easy, Roberta... Why go to the mansion right away?"

"Wixx instructed me to retrieve and destroy an envelope from his office safe in case of an emergency. I can't do that. What if there's another bomb?"

"I'm certain the cops cleared the mansion already. Let me, I'll handle this for you. No one would know. Give me the directions on how to locate the safe."

"I guess that would work? Wixx trusted you also. I would hate to let him down when I promised. With my luck, he'll haunt me."

I grin to myself at Roberta. She's young and impressionable, like I was … never. My childhood didn't afford me the luxury. I learned to not be afraid of the things you cannot see. I found myself too consumed with fearing the visible threats.

Contemplating my motive, perhaps mere curiosity is driving me to the house. Could be I need closure? Or I'm continuing to experience a sense of obligation to Wixx?

I prepare while Billy is in the shower. He'll remain unaware of my leaving and returning. If he knew where I was going, he'd throw a fit. I dress in a pleated skirt and a t-shirt from two years ago. The situation is humorous because now their value has diminished due to changing styles. They would be in a thrift shop by now if the socialites owned them. Thrifting is my jam. Deals give me a rush of excitement. I guess that'll never change. I digress.

I relax on the sofa and start a movie in the entertainment space. I look like I'm settling in for the long haul.

"Gemma? Are you in here?" Billy walks in smelling amazing after his shower. Makes me wish I would have waited for him.

"Yup, gonna chill while you're gone. Still under the weather." Actually, that's true, not lying at all.

He kisses my forehead, likely checking for a temp. "I'll be fine, no fever, I promise."

"OK, you realize I wouldn't leave you…"

"Of course, I remember how sickness became the major focus in your thoughts. Because of your mom."

"Yeah, true. But there's nowhere I'd rather be than taking care of you. I promise, Gem, I've changed my priorities."

"You've shown me that in the past couple of weeks." I grasp his cheeks in my fingers and kiss him on the lips. "I love you. My intention is to resolve matters between us."

"Good, because I have something to confess. Promise you won't get angry." He rubs the back of his neck while stretching the muscles.

"It's OK, Billy, we divorced. No need to reveal the women you've been with."

"NO! I haven't been with anyone. What I did entailed having you sign fake divorce papers. We're still married."

His face gets all scrunched up waiting for some fall out. "I couldn't bear divorcing you, so I fixed it, I'm sorry."

Uncertain if it's the stress of the past twenty-four hours, Wixx's death, or my nausea returning. But I start to cry and laugh simultaneously. He wraps me in his strong embrace, and we laugh in unison.

"Go before the Feds put out a warrant for you." I grin.

"You sure you're not upset?" He wipes my tears with his thumbs.

"We may revisit the topic later, but at this moment, that's all the reaction I have."

He nods. "I love you, Gem. I'll be back as quick as I can."

"Be careful." I wave as he leaves.

As soon as he is out of the gate and the electronic arm closes, I'm out of my seat. I pick the set of keys from the hook displayed in his organized system for his cars. I pause mid step as nausea takes me over and makes me want to vomit again. I run to the bathroom in our bedroom and toss my cookies. As I settle on the floor afterward, I wonder if I might be pregnant. Billy and I had impromptu unprotected sex in the last few weeks. I wasn't in the mindset that I removed my IUD when I quit Innamorare. The device became unnecessary due to the five-year time limit and my decision to abstain from sexual activities. I brush my teeth, rinse, and then rummage through the drawers. Seeking an old pregnancy test from when I hoped a baby would compel Billy to stay home. Thank goodness at the time I came to my senses. But at this moment? I'm not sure?

My fingers touch a box at the back of the towel drawer where I used to hide them. Ripping open the package, I remove the tube and the directions. A deep cleansing breath before proceeding to take the pregnancy test.

Thirty

BILLY

The Feds force me to wait for forty minutes before taking me into the office. They might engage in such behavior to cause you anxiety, but I'm innocent, so I'm okay. One thing I could never do is kill someone over a business deal. It's stupidity.

"Please state your name for the record," Cross says.

"Billy Dedano."

"Mr. Dedano, can you explain your whereabouts yesterday evening?"

"Yes, I was at my club Ice until my friend called and said my wife was at the ball with Wixx. I felt like I wanted to observe them together and assess the relationship, so I was on my way there when Gemma called me to pick her up."

"Gemma is your ex-wife, correct?" Frost asks.

"No, we never got divorced. Just separated. And now back together."

"You had an application for the same license as Wixx at the city council's office, right?"

"Yes, I lost in the meeting last week. It's irrelevant since I've received a lucrative offer for the land compared to what I would have earned from the casino. Also, the buyer will assume all the risk and I will collect a percentage of sales in perpetuity. I'm fortunate enough to invest all my focus with Gemma from this point forward, instead of building the casino. So, win-win."

"That's if you can prove you didn't kill Wixx." Frost threatens.

"One activity I could never engage in is killing someone over a business deal. It's stupidity."

"Well, we view it as motive and the fact that Mr. Wixx was parading your wife around as his new girlfriend. We have eyewitness accounts. They were pretty cozy at the charity ball. He had his hands all over her, and they danced all night." Frost wears a shit-eating grin on his face. I want to punch it off.

"Gemma explained everything to me last night. She was playing a part. Pretending to be his mistress and he was paying her very well."

"Is it something she was quite accustomed to doing at Club Innamorare? Correct?"

"She worked there, yes. What does it matter?"

"We're asking the questions." The younger agent takes off his jacket and folds his arms. Intimidation doesn't work with me. He can turn it off now.

"Did Mr. Wixx ever ask you to launder money through your establishments?"

"In the past, he asked. A request I turned down using language he understood."

"Did he retaliate back then?"

"He's been ever since using various methods. I have always risen above his infantile tactics." I sniff.

Both agents receive text messages at the same instant that seem to rile them. Cross puts his device down on the desk next to me. In my line of sight, I can perceive the message is about Wixx. Frost appears to be answering the text for both of them. Cross continues with the questions.

"How did you and Mr. Wixx meet?" He sits on the edge of the table.

"My father started the company I now own and Wixx tried to manipulate him too. When I took over, he thought I'd be a pushover. I proved him wrong."

Cross's phone blows up again on the desk. He leaves it to Frost to answer while he pours himself a cup of coffee. I read the words…

John: Listening device picking up
disturbance at Wixx residence.

Frost: Who's there?

John: Woman speaking on her phone.
Gemma Dedano.

Frost: She must be telling the staff what
tasks to complete. Disregard.

Cross turns back toward me, and I pull my eyes away. Why would Gemma choose to go back to his place? She promised she'd rest. I need to escape from here.

"Are we finished yet, gentlemen?"

"For now. Don't take any trips, Mr. Dedano." He stands and opens the door.

I rise and grab my jacket off the hook before getting out of there and heading to the Wixx mansion. Gemma needs to have no further association with all this shit. She can acquire a job anywhere.

Gemma's very capable. Hell, if she decides she wants to run one of my clubs, she can. In the past, during our marriage, she never expressed an interest in working. Or maybe she did, and I wasn't paying attention. What the fuck was I doing? I'd been so focused on proving myself to my dad that I'd forgotten how to live. I spent so many years chasing a dream that my father instilled in me. Terrified to think about losing it after he worked so hard to pass it all down to me. I can now delegate responsibilities I once believed only I could manage.

Life exists beyond the clubs, where I can spend quality moments with Gemma and build our own family. That would be pure joy. *How could I lose sight of that? Of her? There's got to be a way to make it up to her. I'm going to dedicate the rest of my life to trying.*

When I arrive at the mansion, the locked gate prevents me from entering and no one is answering the bell. Gem is there, and I won't be put out. Despite the rain, I climb the fence and hop down onto the cobblestone walk. My Audi sits on the circular driveway, getting wet. It's the only car she ever wanted to drive from my collection. Everything looks deserted as I inch up the front steps and ring the bell. After a few minutes, I look through the window to a grand foyer with no one in sight.

Pounding on the window does no good. I even try the handle out of sheer desperation. I decide to walk around and see if I can let Gem know I'm here.

Groundskeepers have fortified the house with bushes and fence to deter intruders. I have to leap over evergreens and hop over a wall to get to the backyard. By the time I make it there, I'm soaked. I slick my hair back with my fingers and brush off my jeans before assessing the entry points. Wixx built this estate right on the shore of Lake Michigan. He has boulders and landscaping to bring out the appealing nature of the shoreline while helping prevent erosion.

I climb the stairs to the large patio where glass-paned doors flank the back of the house. When I peer inside, it's the desolate kitchen. State-of-the-art appliances and furniture quality cabinets sit unused. Moving right, I peer into an empty family room. Then I glimpse her through an open door. My beautiful Gemma is a little further down the line of windows. Balancing on air conditioners is necessary to reach that spot. Playing Spiderman wasn't on my agenda for the day, but here I am.

As I balance on condenser units, Gemma is present, but not alone. I refrain from attracting attention to observe.

Thirty-One

GEMMA

My remote opens the iron gates leading to the curvy driveway of the Wixx mansion. Dark clouds loom over the lake, signaling an impending storm. Huge raindrops are hitting the cobblestones as I reach the shelter of the overhang surrounding the front door. Shit, Billy will notice that the car got rained upon when I return.

My key still works as I let myself into the grand foyer with its marble floors and pillars. A chill runs down my spine whether from the rain or the deserted rooms, I'm not sure. My shoes slip on the floor, so I go back and wipe them on the mat. On my right, the dining room table remains untouched, save for a few misplaced items from the police visit. To my left is the living room. The ambiance is cold and lifeless. I decide I should hurry and get in and out.

Walking down the long hallway to Wixx's office, I consider calling the feds. No one knows I'm here. When I open the door, there's clear chaos everywhere. Someone left drawers open, threw books off the shelves, and even scattered his quick change of clothes from the closet. I must step over debris to enter the area. I push myself to move on. The safe, which is already unlocked, is in plain sight. Nothing is inside and I came here for no reason. This means the cops already confiscated the envelope. I hug myself, rubbing my arms from the chill, when a voice calls from behind me.

"What are you looking for?"

I whirl around, experiencing a wave of dizziness. Things spin around me, stealing my breath from my lungs. A thought enters my brain that I didn't eat all day, right before blackness takes me over.

Awakening on the sofa in the office, I'm unsure of the elapsed time. I shoot up, wondering if what I saw before passing out was real or imagined. My head protests and in response, I close my eyes, clutching my forehead with my fingers. I can sense that I'm not alone when the same presence asks, "Is this what you're looking for?"

Shock takes over, hearing the familiar dulcet tone again, and I tremble inside. My eyes open to find Benjamin Wixx holding up a manila envelope. He displays a big smile on his face, almost as smug as the Cheshire cat in Alice in Wonderland. It's kinda creepy.

Am I being haunted by the ghost of Benjamin Wixx? My throat closes and words aren't an option as I remember Roberta being afraid of this exact scenario. I now have remorse after mocking her childish ignorance in my mind.

"Gemma, are you sick? Why are you so pale? I realize I surprised you, but your reaction is a little over the top. Don't you think?"

"Wha—How are you here?" I manage to form the words through a gravelly tone.

"Simple!" He walks toward me and I cringe backward into the pillows. "Don't be afraid. I merely faked my demise." He sits in front of me on the coffee table. "A brilliant plan to evade prosecution. Don't you agree?"

"I mean, I don't know. Did you kill your driver for effect?" I rub my clammy hands on my skirt.

"Aww, come on Gem, you hated him. Don't tell me you're grieving a sick pervert like him. In fact, in my mind, the day he attacked you sealed his fate."

"You—you killed him for me?" My voice sounds shrill, and I clear my throat to fix the issue.

"Creating a convincing scenario sometimes involves sacrifices. By the time they scrape up the remains from the explosion, we'll be long gone." He runs his fingers down the pleats in his pants, straightening them.

"W—we?"

Wixx flashes a satisfied smile. "Yes, of course. Now that you know I'm alive, you'll be required to vanish together with me. The situation is ideal because now I have a companion. It was clear that we were comfortable together at the ball. Taking you with me is the cherry on top. I'm kind of proud of my master plan, but this new piece is fortuitous."

"No, I can't disappear!" I attempt to rise, but my legs are bound by a chain to a wall-mounted handle.

He gets up and paces. "See, I thought you'd say that. But I cannot afford for you to run away with this important information. So, either you come with me and we live happily ever after … or well…" He shrugs. "You can be collateral damage, just like poor Ronald. Your choice."

"You cannot do this!" There's a pounding in my ears. "This is a case of kidnapping!"

"Who's to stop me?" He laughs. "Now be a good girl and cooperate."

Without a doubt, I have no choice here. No one is aware of my location. Come on, Gem, you're self-reliant. You can escape from this situation alive. An idea comes to mind. I might just act friendly and pretend I'm interested in going. This way he may unshackle me and I have a chance. I relax my posture and my face.

“Where are we going?” I inquire in a more composed manner.

“Not sure yet. I have a transport leaving from Arizona into Mexico tomorrow to pick up a load. Maybe we will join.” He’s ruffling through papers on the desk. “Such a mess. The cops have no respect.”

This man has lost his sanity. I need as much information as I can gather out of him. “But how will we fly to Arizona within the timeframe?”

“Don’t concern yourself with the specifics, darling. The experience will be enjoyable. I’ll be right back.” He leaves without a look back at me.

I rise, careful not to fall, and check to see if perhaps he left the keys on the desk. No luck. He’s also placed my bag with my phone inside on the bookcase across the office from me. The chains rattle as I search for a weapon I can conceal, but there’s nothing. I check the drawers to find a letter opener. No such luck. The moment I untangle the chain from my ankles and sit back on the couch, Wixx returns holding two sandwiches and a glass of lemonade.

“We have to eat before we leave. How long we’ll be on the road is undetermined.” He sets mine on the coffee table in front of me.

“I need to let my friend Regina know I’m going out of town.” I shrug, trying to act as nonchalant as possible. “She will be worried and most likely call the police.”

“Nonsense. You have no family to miss you, and friends easily forget. Eat your sandwich and we will leave.”

My body needs food, so I won’t argue. While I chew, I decide not to allow him to take me to another location, just as the self-defense class taught me. When he unshackles my ankle, I intend to knee him in the nose or the balls. That is my only hope.

He walks back and forth on the fancy silk rug, avoiding trash and gathering important items like passports, money, and the envelope that got me into trouble. What the hell does the damn thing contain?

Thirty-Two

BILLY

When I first see Gemma, the open safe on the wall covers her head, but that ass is a sexy sight. Fear interrupts my admiration when she turns and passes out. I try the latch on the window with all my might. It's locked. Then I climb back to the patio. Upon reaching there and looking through the window, she's gone.

She may have stood up. I try all the doors, to no avail. I climb onto the air conditioner again in order to have a clearer view. Gem lies on the sofa, unconscious. The shocker? Benny the con artist is standing over her dressed as Benjamin Wixx. Why haven't the authorities caught on to this yet?

I grab my phone and the card in my wallet. I text Agent Cross about the situation.

Billy: The asshole faked his death ... Wixx is alive and at his mansion with Gemma. She's unconscious. I can't access the place.

Cross: We saw on the hidden cameras ... they are in the office. We sent out the SWAT team in case of a hostage situation. They are minutes out ... DO NOT ENGAGE! Wait for us to arrive.

This is just another attempt of Benny Soto reinventing himself. No wonder Gem passed out in shock. I must make my way inside. I won't risk her safety. Right now, she's not a threat to him, so he wouldn't hurt her. Yet. Gemma can be a firecracker and if she becomes confrontational, the situation has the potential to turn dangerous.

When I secure a position to see into the window again, Gem is awake and speaking calmly, not her usual actions when she's threatened. The impression is that she is being agreeable to please him. Something deep inside me questions Gem's motivation for being here.

Is she an accomplice to the crime?

Did he somehow blackmail her into helping him fake his death?

If so, she'd be the only individual who knows he's still breathing. This is a threat to him, requiring him to eliminate her as a witness.

Would he kill her? Tunnel vision comes over me.

With that realization, I almost fall off the piece of equipment I'm balancing on. Jumping to the patio, I desperately search for a way inside, circling the home and attempting every entrance and window. Everything is locked up tight until I try the garage service door. It's open.

I walk among his collection of rare automobiles that rival my own. Automatic lights activate when I approach the front. A tire iron is on the bench, and on instinct I reach for the tool. Since I was with the Feds being questioned, I came here without my gun. I enter the kitchen and then maneuver to the study through the unlocked door. The hallway stretches out, adorned with hardwood floors and a soft carpet runner that quiets my steps. I'm able to remain just outside and listen.

"I need to inform my friend Regina that I'm going out of town." Gemma says.

"Nonsense. There is no family to miss you, and friends easily forget. In my personal experience, reshaping oneself can be as rejuvenating as a palate cleanser. I can shed all the baggage that seems to cling to me somehow because I am super rich. And I can use my money to create a new identity, different and exhilarating. This time, the sole contrast is that I have to disappear without a trace. Eat your sandwich and we will leave."

"I'm without a passport. You can't remove me from the country." It seems Gem is trying everything to persuade him to free her.

"On the contrary, my dear. I can take you anywhere I please. You can never re-enter the country without me."

"Please Ben, can I leave and pack some of my things? I can grab my passport and you won't need to exert additional effort."

"Don't you worry, my little one. We are about to embark on an adventure together and I will provide you with every luxury, I assure you. Now I will step into the closet to change and while I'm gone think of the sandy beaches we will lazy on for the rest of our lives together. You will learn to be a nice little companion, even though you're not getting paid for your services."

"I'd like to change as well. Can I bring the clothes that are in my office? I promise I won't go anywhere if you release me."

"Regrettably, sweetheart, that cannot be done. I will confine you until I'm sure we agree on our relationship status."

When Wixx goes into the closet to change, I peek inside the room. Gem is not there of her own accord; she has shackles on her ankles. She can remain upright, but the chains only reach so far. I wave at her. When she catches sight of me, tears well up in her eyes. I shake my head, telling her to remain composed without using words. I position myself on the opposite side, observing them in the window's reflection.

Wixx pauses while he picks up a photograph. "This commemorates my first experience of my reincarnation. The occurrence took place when I returned from prison. After I was incarcerated, my family and friends, except for my mother, wanted nothing to do with me. I demonstrated to them my ability to undergo such a metamorphosis that they would seek my attention with desperation. And you know? Some came around, but how can I expect loyalty from those who abandoned me? The experience was cathartic, though, to shun them as they had me. They are weak, unimportant details I forgot to remember in my rise to billionaire status."

"Do you consider them weak because you feel they lacked the courage to act against the law as you so perfected?"

"Yes! You understand me like no other. Is this because you were married to the one person who is the antithesis of what I stand for? Gemma, did you leave him because you found it difficult to bear living up to his superior moral ground?"

"If you want to discuss weakness or lack thereof? Billy is the most remarkable individual I will ever encounter. He upholds elevated moral standards while achieving success in every facet of life."

Hearing Gem standing up for me against him makes me proud. But I fear how he will react in the next few seconds. I prepare to pounce, can't wait anymore for the Feds.

Wixx throws the frame at the fireplace, causing the glass to shatter. "His high and mighty attitude, he thinks he has the formula for success. Fuck that! I did it in years' less time." He pulls Gem up from the sofa and turns her so her back is to his chest and his hand upon her throat. "And now I'm getting you! So, I win." He pushes her forward over the desk, her beautiful hair covering her face. "Soon you'll be bending over like this, begging me to fuck you. In the same way that you gave in to my charms when we kissed earlier."

Thirty-Three

GEMMA

I can't believe Billy just heard Wixx say I kissed him. I'm no saint, that's for sure, and he's aware of that. But we've been making such progress. After his declaration of fidelity and the fake divorce papers, he must be experiencing such a sense of betrayal. I wouldn't blame him if he walked away and left me to be brutalized and taken.

Wixx holds me folded over his desk with his erection poking me in the ass. He grips my throat, holds my wrists behind my back with his other hand, and there are shackles around my ankles. I'm at his mercy. If Billy were not present to listen to us, I would proceed with Wixx and be agreeable to gain ground. It had been working earlier... not sufficient to persuade him to set me free, but he refrained from attacking me. Somehow, knowing my man is here to save me made me bold, and I ticked off the asshole. Now, I must run with it.

"I'll never beg you for anything! Whatever attention you desire, you will need to extract it from me with force." I struggle in his grasp.

"Why the sudden change in attitude? You don't fuck billionaires at will anymore? Guess you no longer excel at your job. I received information that in the past you were the best." He sniffs my hair. "How about we engage in a little fun on my desk? I've been patient, waiting to discover firsthand." His palm travels up my thigh to the side of my thong panties and over the globe of my ass.

"Stop! You fucking pervert! Get your paws off me!" My reaction is to head butt him in the nose since he released my neck. I give it a shot and only make contact with air.

I'm surprised when he listens to me and his grip falls away. Even the one on my wrists behind my back is gone. During my screaming, I may have overlooked the grunt from Billy as he struck Wixx over the skull with a tire iron.

"Gem! Are you okay? Sorry, I moved down the hall momentarily because I heard something in the other part of the house." He grabs me in his arms. I hug him and turn to kick Wixx in the shoulder while he's sprawled out on the ground.

Billy laughs, "Little bit of vengeance, my love?"

"You bet your ass! I cooperated with what he wanted to make progress and convince him to release me. But as soon as I saw you, I said fuck that." I slap my arms around his neck.

"Fuck that! This asshole is going down, the cops are almost he…"

His sentence is cut short when Wixx grabs Billy from behind, blood dripping down his face. He has him in a choke hold. Wixx is no match for strength and Billy strikes backward with his elbow to the ribs. Sufficient to make the weaker of the two release their grip. Punches are flying, and I evade the fallout by bracing myself against the bookcases. Billy throws a powerful kick to the ribs and Wixx falls at my feet. His prize bronze horse statue is right above me—how fitting when I grab hold of the object and end the fight with a gash to his head, knocking him out cold. Strangely, I hear screaming and I'm shocked to find out that the source is me.

The SWAT team closes in, putting the cuffs on before the EMT passes the smelling salts under his nose. He wakes with a start, shouting at Billy.

"You motherfucker! Think you can do away with me? Nobody can stop me. I'll be back, just like last time. You'll see! I was winning, I had the advantage. She was under my control. Ask her! We had stuff between us. Once a slut, always a slut!" The cops pull Wixx up to his feet by his handcuffs behind his back while he protests in a futile attempt to shake them off.

"You're delusional! I can't wait to testify and put you away…" Billy grabs me in a fierce way to shut me up. "I don't care. He's a scumbag." No one hears me but him. They are already outside in the rain, putting Wixx into the squad car.

"Calm down Gem, it's all over. You're safe and we can return home." He's rubbing my arms, attempting to make me focus.

"Thank you for coming. I can't imagine what I would have done without you." I kiss him on the lips.

"Let's hope you never have to find out." He puts his arm around me and we leave the mess behind.

While driving, Billy is quiet. At some point, I'm certain I should explain myself. I keep wondering if I should start now. The optimal course of action is to find out his thoughts. Get things out in the open.

"I can hear the gears grinding in that gorgeous brain of yours." He says.

"Well, I thought I should explain a few things." I place my hand over his.

"Why the fuck did you kiss him and let him put his hands all over you? I mean, I'm trying to convince myself that you were just playing the part. Yet, all of this was completely unnecessary. If you stayed with me and worked things out, you wouldn't have needed a job, hence no working for Wixx."

I remove my hand. "We're back to you wanting me to stay home and wait around for my money machine to come home and play?"

He pulls into his lavish garage, the spot where I took the Audi from, still empty. I don't care how or if he ever gets it back. Fuming, I jump out before he makes a complete stop. I kick the door of the stupid shiny car next to me and enter the elevator, not waiting for him. When the doors close, I scream as loud as I can into the mirror. The act provides a cathartic release, and given what I've endured, there's a compelling urge to release the anger.

Once in the bedroom, I rip off my clothes and slip on his t-shirt. I climb into bed and face the wall. His footsteps are close and the bed dips as he gets on. "I made a mistake and expressed all of my emotions with inaccuracy. Jealousy overwhelmed me and I regret my actions. I understand you didn't need my 'I told you so' after everything you've been through."

Thirty-Four

BILLY

She sniffles, turning around in the bed to face me. Her eyes are bloodshot and sunken. "Are we never getting past this? Because I can't be happy here with you if we don't agree."

"No, Gem, that's not ... I was concerned about you. I'm aware of what a piece of shit Wixx is, and you were in his clutches. I kept trying to tell myself you could take care of yourself. But he had the potential to harm you if I wasn't there. It doesn't mean I can't agree with you having a career. Just not with someone the likes of Benjamin Wixx."

She moves to her knees, wiping her face with her palms. "I'm sorry too. It must have been painful to hear him say that I kissed him. My intention was to make him trust me for the purpose of planting the cameras and listening devices."

I grab both her hands in mine, nodding. "Tomorrow, we talk to Eve and Maria and find you another job."

"You mean it? You're OK with it?"

"Of course, all I know is I never want to be without you in my bed ever again."

She giggles and tackles me to my back. She straddles me, her hands on my chest.

"I'm saying yes!" She smiles big.

"Yes, is a good thing to say … anything in particular it pertains to?"

"Moving back in here. You've shown me I've become your top priority by finding me at Wixx's mansion. How did you figure it out?"

"I overheard on agent Frost's cell that the surveillance crew picked you up in his office. I ended the interrogation and came right away."

"Well, I'm glad you did. You saved us from harm, and I believe it's enough to forgive and forget the past. Just remember, though, if you revert … It won't be pretty." She digs her index finger into my pec.

"Ow! What do you mean us?" My eyebrows cinch together.

"Oh, I forgot to tell you in all the commotion … Ummm…" She bites the nail on her pinky finger.

"What did you forget? I'll tickle it out of you like I used to…" I roll us over and poke her sides. She squirms and laughs. Her face getting red.

"OK, stop! I'll tell you! You're going to be a daddy."

"What! I am?—We are?" I point to each of us. Gem nods with another dazzling smile on her face. "Holy shit! I love you!"

My kisses are now more passionate and complete than ever before. Her mouth is warm and her lips are cool as she kisses me back, making me hotter than ever. I stand at the side of the bed, looking over her as she smiles up at me. Gem is the most stunning woman I've ever seen with her golden hair fanned out on the white bedding; blue eyes sparkling. They say when women are pregnant; they glow. My gem is glowing like the sun, just for me.

My heart beat drums in my erection as I shove down my jeans and pull my shirt over my head. She peruses my naked body while licking her lips and moaning. Then she sits up and whips off the t-shirt, shaking out her curls. The sight almost makes me lose it already. Sitting on her knees, she arches her spine, perching on all fours. The dip of her spine, the crack of her ass, leading to her pretty pink pussy, blows my fucking mind. Her lips burn just as pink, swollen from our kisses, when she glances back at me over her shoulder.

"Naughty girl, you want it from behind?" Her teeth indent the rosy flesh as she bites her lip. "It's just for starters." She giggles. I clamp one hand on her hip and the other on my cock. Yanking her backward, I line up perfectly. She rocks back, sliding down my length.

"More! Fuck me, Billy." When I oblige, her spine rolls, her head folding toward the bed. I lean forward, wrapping my arm around her chest and fondling her dangling tits, squeezing the weight. My kisses hot on her spine as I thrust over and over, bringing us both to the heights of bliss.

She's tucked under my arm, her cheek resting on my chest. Our breathing has returned to normal and we're enjoying the afterglow. "You were holding back at first because of the baby, right?"

"Well, maybe … subconsciously." I clear my throat.

"Our little nugget is safe and sound protected by my womb. Having sex won't hurt him or her. I looked it up when I found out I was pregnant." She rubs her smooth, flat stomach.

I squeeze her tight. "That is fucking good to know!"

"I'm going to make an appointment to see the doctor." Gem turns and perches on her elbows to look me in the eye. "Will you go with me?"

"Baby, I'm here for you. Whatever you want or need … I'm your guy."

"Even if I start craving weird food and send you out in the middle of the night?" She bites her lip.

"Yup, you and the nugget are my only priority from now until forever. I promise."

"What about the lakefront project? You might get the license since Wixx is in jail."

I rub her back with my fingertips. "Joe has already procured a buyer, and I'm making more than enough profit to satisfy. I'm giving my job to Andrew. He's someone I can trust, and he has the time to take on the responsibilities I used to work on full time."

"When did you do all this?" She rests back on my chest.

"I did it on the day I promised you I would make you my person of greatest importance." My arms surround her, squeezing tighter than ever.

"Oh shit, you mean it? I have never loved you more than I do right now." She squeezes me back.

"Wait until you have me home with you twenty-four hours a day … you might want to send me back to work."

"Nope, because we already decided that we'll talk to Eve and Maria tomorrow. I'll be at my job and you can stay home and wait for me." Gem smiles against my skin.

"I'm fine with it until the baby comes and you better take off some time to bond."

"Of course, that goes without saying."

"I decided to donate some of my car collection to charity. While I'm waiting for you here, I'll be researching organizations who need help." She gets back up on her knees, her eyebrows hitting her hairline.

"That sounds amazing! Why stop there? I always wanted to create a resource for underprivileged women who need clothes to go to interviews and to work after they're hired. I came up with the idea when I went into my closet and saw you never gave away my clothes."

"Baby, I never gave away your clothes because I never accepted the fact that you left." I roll to my side and balance on my elbow.

"Obviously, since you made me sign fake divorce papers." She slaps my shoulder.

"I apologized, and aren't you glad now?" I caress her cheek with my fingertips.

"Well, it would have been fun to get married again. You know? Vows and everything." She draws a heart on my chest with her fingernail.

"Aw, baby, I vow to love you, cherish you and provide orgasms every day." We giggle.

She jumps up and heads to the bathroom. "Now come wash my back, among other things." She looks back at me and pops up her foot behind her.

"My Gem, she's insatiable."

It's odd. When you feel like you're at a crossroads, it may be a sign from the universe indicating the need to stop engaging in activities that don't bring you joy, and focus on prioritizing the ones that do. All the things I've built in my life so far are a feat few can achieve. But this family we're building, even though others do it daily, is undoubtedly our greatest undertaking. Gemma and I are building a new foundation, a stronger one—a foundation that will jumpstart the next chapter in our lives.

Thirty-Five

GEMMA

It's a beautiful day and Eve and I are shopping for baby clothes. There's something irresistible about tiny human clothing that you just can't stop smiling. I hold up a onesie with the words I'm the oldest. Whoa, I can't wrap my mind around having a sibling yet.

"Billy and I chose the baby's room as the one across the hall from ours. The rooms don't share a wall for when we get crazy in bed," I wink.

"I always say, never wake a sleeping baby!" Eve laughs. "You'll be surprised how much you'll want to change your sex life when the baby comes, primarily because of exhaustion. But don't give in to it. I have a secret rule of keeping a happy marriage." Her voice lowers in volume.

"Ooh, do tell." I lock my arm with hers as we walk.

"I never decline when Ian desires lovemaking. And I initiate it first on regular occasions, no matter how tired I am from the twins. We even take it off campus, if you catch my drift." She smiles. "It works!"

"Very sound advice. I'll keep that in mind."

My stomach is rumbling, so we go to a bistro near the mall for lunch. The view of the city from the patio is breathtaking, with the skyscrapers.

"There's the location of my past interview with Wixx." I point to Willis Tower. "I remember being so nervous and wondering if my shoes were too slutty."

Eve laughs, "Ian says Benjamin Wixx or Benny Soto is going to prison for a long time."

"Yeah, I have to testify about the manilla envelope I was retrieving from his office when he played his resurrection trick on me. To indict him and the wealthy individuals he blackmailed, we must establish a chain of custody. The envelope contained many famous people." I whisper the last part.

"It's the only way those people would trust him with their money. It was extortion."

"Good thing Ian had nothing to hide when Wixx pursued him. You know, he requested me to have you recommend him to Ian." I play with a piece of lettuce in my salad with my fork. "Just between you and me … I can understand how Wixx could reel a person in with his charm. He carried it out on me on several occasions. I told myself that I was going along with his advances to further the case for the feds. To be honest, I found myself attracted to him for a minute, until he revealed his narcissistic true colors the next.

"Don't beat yourself up about that." She places her palm over mine on the table. "I picked up on that at the charity ball, but only because I know you so well. There are men that have that natural charisma and the bad boy alpha element is kinda sexy sometimes. Even Ian has it. But narcissism is where I draw the line." Her mouth twists.

"Yeah, now I just want to put him away. Get him off the streets." Eve nods and takes a sip of her drink.

"How do you feel about Billy turning down the Casino license? The board was apologetic about having a member who took bribes."

"It's just another manner he is putting us first." I place my palm on my stomach.

"Well? Are you sharing with me what you're having?" She blots her lipstick with her napkin.

I put down my fork and push my plate an inch. "I can't. Billy is still in the dark."

"Wasn't he with you when you had the ultrasound?" Her head tilts.

"Yes, and we talked about being surprised. But later I couldn't help myself and I looked at the file." I shrug.

"There are perks to working for the top OBGYN in the country. And being her best friend, too."

"Thanks again for finding me the most incredible job ever." I blow her an imaginary kiss.

"You're welcome!"

Eve parks in our drive and gets out to help me with all the bags. When we enter the house, Billy is nowhere to be found when I call his name. Placing the shopping haul in the baby's room, we return to the kitchen and spot his note. I pull it from the fridge and read it aloud.

"*Meet me in the gazebo.*"

Eve and I exchange a look of wonder, then go to the yard. Once we step onto the deck, Eve joins the chorus of surprise. I'm taken aback until Eve takes me by the hand and leads me through the guests to the gazebo. A guitar begins to play the song Billy proposed to me with. This reenactment replicates the entire event from years ago in Las Vegas. Minus the male strippers, I giggle to myself.

The song lingers through the surrounding speakers when he puts down his guitar and kneels before me. His brown eyes are sparkling with love.

"Gemma Bloom Dedano, will you grant me the honor of being the luckiest guy on the planet and be my wife for the second time?" He takes my hand.

I pull him up and throw my arms around his neck. "Yes, a thousand times. Yes!" The guests all cheer. I plant a passionate kiss on him and then wipe my lipstick off his lips with my thumbs.

"Preacher, come marry us one more time," Billy yells.

A gentleman in a suit comes walking up to us from the pool house. The guests quiet down. We turn, standing side by side as he begins with dearly beloved. By the time he pronounces us husband and wife, we've said vows and proclaimed our undying love for one another. The crowd cheers again as Billy swirls me into a deep dip with a panty melting kiss.

"Were you surprised?" He asks. "I've been planning this for weeks and was worried you would find out."

"I was shocked. You went through all this trouble for me."

"Baby, my life is about pleasing you from now until eternity. Because I love you more than anything." We kiss. "When you told me you wanted another wedding … the wheels up here…" He points to his brain. "started turning to execute this all. I wanted it to be your style, all casual and warm."

"Well, it's perfect, thank you."

Food trucks set up in the drive and a chef grills steaks and hamburgers on the barbecue. A full bar with a champagne tower and a dessert table with my favorite melted chocolate fountain, donuts, and chocolate chip cookies. He went the extra mile and remembered to purchase supplies for s'mores by the bonfire after we ate, danced and partied.

Despite resembling a children's birthday gathering, my man now comprehends my preference for simplicity. The DJ plays some country favorites and typical wedding songs while our friends are all dancing and drinking.

"Eve, where are the guys?"

"Ian just said he'd be back in a moment." She hands me another glass of bubbly. "Did you notice Maria and Aaden?"

"Yeah, they just flew back from visiting the in-laws in Greece. She invited us to accompany them next trip." I fake clap, watching not to spill.

"She included us in the invite!" Eve toasts me with her champagne glass.

"That will be a shitload of fun. I've only traveled to Vegas." I see Maria heading toward us.

"Hey, here are my girls! Aaden ditched me to venture somewhere with the guys." Maria puts her arms on each of our shoulders and starts bopping us to the dance floor. We continue dancing and walking right along to the middle to join the line dance. Everybody's doing the Cupid Shuffle, and we shove in and step in unison.

After the shuffle music ends, the darkness envelops us. With only moonlight illuminating our surroundings, an unexpected spotlight shines on the gazebo. All our guys are standing in a triangle formation in the middle of the platform. There's Billy in his grey sweatpants and hoody at the point. The smooth voice of Ginuwine accompanies the slick track of My Pony as he starts his choreography.

"OH MY GOD! Do you see what I'm seeing?" Eve screams. "How the fuck did he drag Ian up there? No way!" She runs to get to the front.

"Come on, let's get closer." Maria says. "I'm taking video for posterity."

We all navigate our path to the front, and everyone is screaming. I'm the loudest of all. The friends are all in sync around Billy, doing his usual moves to the song. When the crescendo sounds, they remove their t-shirts on cue all together. The crowd goes wild. Some of the girls from the club throw their bikini tops at them. Now it's a free for all and my Billy is in the middle, relishing every minute. Once he spots me, though, nothing diverts his attention for the entire rest of the performance. Even topless women.

Intense eye contact and seductive moves? Yes, please.

Epilogue

GEMMA

There's something about pregnancy that makes men into baby talking overprotective idiots. I know what you're thinking … I should embrace the attention I so yearned for at the beginning. And I promise I'm loving every minute of Billy whispering sweet nothings to my belly and waiting for me. He dropped me off at my job today. Eve's friend at the hospital, Dr. Cerelia Amici, is a gynecologist and fertility specialist. She was looking for an office manager and I'm the perfect candidate.

It's been five months since I started and together, we've accomplished so many projects. Using the funds generated by the necklace Wixx gave me, she and I embraced my concept of pre-owned garments. We applied it to the unwed new mothers Cerelia works with when they deliver their babies. She gives them high end obstetric care pro bono. Then we assist them in securing job interviews, provide them with stylish clothing to enhance their confidence, and help them get back on their feet. I never realized the practical applications available to us when we use our wealth for positive purposes. It makes me appreciate all the hard work Billy has invested to reach this point, and the charity he's supported since.

"Good morning, Dr. A. The waiting room is filling up. I put your coffee and the papers you requested on your desk." I say, as I sit ready to give her an update.

"Thank you, Gemma. You have lived up to your name by simplifying my life in the past few months. You anticipate my every need and are a true gem."

"Aww, thanks Dr. A. It's my pleasure. I love working here and I'm in the right place to bring this baby into the world."

"When the moment arrives, we'll be prepared," she says, putting on her white coat and smoothing down the collar. After savoring her first sip of coffee, she sits behind the desk and we begin, just as we do every day. "I'm ready. Update me."

"Mrs. Correlle is first up and she is having break through bleeding. Then there's a hot lawyer waiting to ask you questions about the Baxter legal matter."

"That's interesting …" She gets up and heads to the sign-in counter to scope it out. She picks up a few folders and returns. "I've met him at Eve's wedding. And before that, he was a bachelor in our charity date raffle. Eve once told me that Ian said Joe wanted to bid on me at the raffle, but I got called away to an emergency C Section."

"He never asked you out after the wedding?" I put down my clipboard.

"By the time the wedding that didn't happen was over and Eve had the babies, it was too late. That day was total chaos. My top priority was the welfare of the twins and Eve. I guess it wasn't meant to be."

"Oh, yeah, Eve's water broke just as she was about to walk down the aisle." Cerelia nods. "Well, timing is everything. If I were you, I'd jump that man now."

"Nah, Eve told me he's one of those confirmed forever bachelors. No matter how hot he may be, I don't have time to waste on that shit. Let's get to work. I'll fit him in after Mrs. Correlle."

I watch as Cerelia escorts Joe Costa into her office and offers him something to drink. They are both smiling and being cordial. Hell, they are a handsome couple as they walk next to each other.

I can't help but wonder if fate is laughing at her right now.

Our choices change the trajectory of events.

Eve's prior choice to leave the charity ball was necessary.

Is this Dr. Cerelia Amici's fate coming full circle face to face with her once again? Is it meant to be that Joe and Cerelia should be together?

All I can say is I fucked up my fate for a few years. Thank goodness the symbolic scroll, the almighty, or whatever celestial being controls that shit took pity on me. My universe is back on its axis and Billy, the baby, and I will live happily ever after.

HERE'S YOUR NEXT READ...

A Brush with Obsession is a romantic suspense story with a fierce heroine.

"He exuded self-confidence, but minus the oversized ego, I would call it power, a silent all-consuming power."

Samantha finally finds her soul mate. A stalker wants them both dead. Can she stop the killer's plan & get her happily ever after or is this the end?

A BRUSH WITH OBSESSION

The FALL FROM GRACE series will continue in book #4 PRODIGAL BACHELOR.

Cerelia and Joe become partners in fighting crime. A fake marriage is necessary to fool the criminals. But they can't deny something is sizzling between them. Something hot and completely unexpected.

And it might just be getting a little too real.

WATCH FOR UPDATES >

Newsletter

BONUS

It's Mia's wedding day, but she is in love with another man. Will deception last forever, or will she be forced to make a deadly choice?

The Misconception of Mia.

Read it FREE by using the QR code on the last page of this book.

Reviews are crucial when it comes to assisting fellow readers choose their next book. You can help them by just leaving a few sentences about this book as a REVIEW.

REVIEWS FOR PRODIGAL EX

About the Author

Theresa is blessed to be married to her main man for thirty-seven years. She knows what it takes to have a loving, lasting relationship. Her husband keeps her laughing after all this time. Tips on keeping the sparks alive along with the witty banter appear in her writing regularly. Her tagline "Add some spice to your life, read Romance" is a clever way of describing the feelings her writing evokes.

Love stories, a little suspense, and the happily ever after are Theresa's prescription to keep you smiling. She is ecstatic to share her characters with the world and entertain her readers. Her big Italian family extends throughout the country with a rich and flavorful history. Much of that history spurs ideas for the stories she creates. Make sure you visit the *Art Imitates Life* in the back of every one of her books. It's fun to see where ideas are born.

If you enjoyed reading *this book*. See more of all the characters in Theresa's fictional world. Use the QR code below.

WEBSITE

tiktok.com/@theresapaparomanceauthor
instagram.com/theresapapa_author
amazon.com/author/theresapapa
facebook.com/authortheresapapa
bookbub.com/authors/theresa-papa

"Art Imitates Life"

'Art imitates life' is true about certain details in the story you read. It might be interesting for you to know some of the elements that are somewhat born out of reality.

· By now, you most likely figured out the song that spurred Gemma on when she wrecked Billy's cars is the amazing Carrie Underwood song, 'Before He Cheats'.

· The fact that Billy loves cars and collects them comes from my younger years, when my father would collect antique cars. It was a hobby of his to buy and fix them up and sell them looking brand new. When I became driving age, he gave me a 1956 thunderbird convertible. The color was a vibrant pink!

· The restaurant Benjamin Wixx takes Gemma to for lunch is on top of Willis Tower in Chicago. Growing up in Illinois, I knew it as The Sears Tower, but alas, time changes all.

· The way I wrote the scene where Gemma realizes Billy is the person behind all of her confidence comes from the reality of my husband. He is the driving force behind all of my ability to go on each day living through chronic illness. He gives me the confidence to put my stories out into the world.

· When Gemma mentions she learned to overcome fear of the invisible... In truth, my mother-in-law used to advise, 'Fear not the unseen. It's the things you can see to be frightened of.' (In context, she used to joke about coming back to visit us after she passed. And I said not to come to me because I would lose my shit. In her own way, she meant that it's more logical to fear living threats than a loved one's spirit.)

· The part where Gemma talks about thrifting and loving a deal.... Comes from my daughter.

· The restaurant that Billy takes Gemma to on the first date is real. The entire restaurant is in the kitchen. Here's a quote from their website... *"At Roister, we've built our kitchens to be the restaurant. We elevate comforting, rustic dishes with fine dining techniques and global flavors. The results are a combination of understated platings and vibrant flavors."*

Bonus

DON'T FORGET…

Get your FREE prequel to The Connected Series. The Misconception of Mia Use the QR code below or

CLICK HERE.

FREE BOOK!

www.ingramcontent.com/pod-product-compliance
Lightning Source LLC
LaVergne TN
LVHW010551160826
845677LV00013B/3079
* 9 7 9 8 9 8 5 1 4 9 8 3 8 *